Gablet - The Game of Dreams

I0418834

Evincepub
Publishing

Evincepub Publishing

Parijat Extension, Bilaspur, Chhattisgarh 495001

First Published by Evincepub Publishing 2017

Copyright Lavina Chhabra © 2017

All Rights Reserved.

ISBN: 978-1-5457-1660-1

Price: Rs.290/-

This book has been published with all reasonable efforts taken to make the material error-free after the consent of the author. No part of this book shall be used, reproduced in any manner whatsoever without written permission from the author, except in the case of brief quotations embodied in critical articles and reviews. The Author of this book is solely responsible and liable for its content including but not limited to the views, representations, descriptions, statements, information, opinions and references ["Content"]. The Content of this book shall not constitute or be construed or deemed to reflect the opinion or expression of the Publisher or Editor. Neither the Publisher nor Editor endorse or approve the Content of this book or guarantee the reliability, accuracy or completeness of the Content published herein and do not make any representations or warranties of any kind, express or implied, including but not limited to the implied warranties of merchantability, fitness for a particular purpose. The Publisher and Editor shall not be liable whatsoever for any errors, omissions, whether such errors or omissions result from negligence, accident, or any other cause or claims for loss or damages of any kind, including without limitation, indirect or consequential loss or damage arising out of use, inability to use, or about the reliability, accuracy or sufficiency of the information contained in this book.

Gablet

The Game of Dreams

Lavina Chhabra

ACKNOWLEDGMENT

I would like to thank my mother for giving me all the support I needed, JyotsnaBhambhani, for being my editor in crime, all the good people around me who kept me motivated, and animals, who have always loved me unconditionally.

ABOUT THE AUTHOR

Born in 1993, she was brought up in India. With a background of science, and a heart of arts, she works as a designer at day, and a writer at night. She has been active in helping injured animals around her, with a passion for all animals. She loves to travel, capture moments in camera, play instruments, and whatever keeps her lively.

PART 1

1.

I look at the green shining circle of light. The savior from darkness. Moon, defined as the signature of love. The green light is reflecting on my green skin. Giving my green body a darker shade of green. It is known and unknown at the same time. I am myself and something else. I know this place. I know this window. Still, this is new to me. I walk out of the green room. *My* green room. Walk away from my house. *My* green house. Finding the street to have the same green shades of harmony. The color of balance in life. The color that is an indication of equilibrium of mind and heart. How this is equilibrium for me, is unknown to me.

I look around myself. Everything is the color of balance, everything is wrapped in green. Is the Earth still balanced? Or am I hallucinating its existence? My life is a ruin at the moment. Why the balance then?

I walk towards his house. His empty green house. The red door is replaced by a green one. Anger is replaced by harmony. The white body of the house is replaced by evil green. The loneliness is replaced by harmony. My heart aches. The pinch in it takes me to the colorful world of red, black and red. The world of rage, abyss and love.

Where am I? What is this place? What is this commotion?

I hear the sound of footsteps. Not mine. Not any human's. Not any living animals'. Whose is it then? I stand at the center of the road, try to solve the mystery of myself. What is going on in my head? What do I want from myself?

I know what it is. The footsteps. The commotion. I can see it. Approaching towards me. The huge green colored. This time it is not depicting calmness. Rather, it is my fear. My greatest fear. I am standing still. Where would I run? Into the green houses? Into my green house which is not mine anymore?

It is approaching me at apace. I feel time relativity around me. It's coming slow, but for me, it's running towards me. Left. Right. Left. Right. The footsteps are more like tremors. Still, I stand like a statue of harmony, without any harmony. My greatest fear is approaching towards me, and it is this fear that has stilled me. Unable to move a single muscle of my green body.

Dinosaur! Its slimy skin is beckoning me. Its reptile-y eyes are dilating at my sight. Its shades are shining on my green skin like a warning signal. *I am going to die*. My fear is going to kill me. My fear will win and the harmony will lose. The war is on!

This STEGOSAURUS is gonna have millions of fans on YouTube. I am amused on my handling of fear. I am rather confused whether I should run, or should I be memorized as the dinosaur girl by my millions of future fans on YouTube by taking a video.

I end up doing neither and staring at its miraculously scary structure. What a creature it is! Some study them, while some are Ornithoscelidaphobic like me. I admire paleontologists. The work they do, researching about the Earth's history is a colossal task.

He is standing 20 feet from me, giving me the same look that I am giving him. The look of an alien. The look when one has lost everything of one owns. The look which describes the longing for someone in your life. *What is he longing for? His family? Food? Am I his food? Is he going to eat me and then laugh, and say 'What a skinny reckless flesh!'? What does he want from me?* Oh! 'It' has changed to 'he' now? *Do I empathize him? I mean 'it'? Is he me from inside?*

I keep aside my empathy or whatever I feel for him and move forward towards him. He is standing still, scrutinizing my footsteps, not tremors, unlike his. His eyes are beautiful, and scary. He could eat me up whole. *A green skinny girl inside a green fat giant.* I giggle and step forward where I can see every trough and peak on his slimy skin. I can see his numerous plates depicting his elegance in nature. I can see him standing 10 feet above me. His eyes are glued on a single thing. His prey. Or his mirage?

I find my conscious whispering a secret in my ears. Revealing the truth about the false. The thing that would open up my path of life. I open my mouth and spit on his green paw. Right giant paw. It is not the green liquid that has built its home in our mouths. It is a green shiny medicine-like sphere. It has the radius of not more than a centimeter. It touches his paw and burst into the real colors of flames, making my world colorful again, breaking my world form the balance again, and bringing me to the artificial reality of life.

The dinosaur reacts on the blast. Every action has an equal and opposite reaction.

He is falling on me. *Now I am* really *going to die.*

2.

"Rachel"

"RACHEL!"

"WAKE UP, Rachel"

Urgh! My mom always brings me to the real practical world.

"I am up mom. Stop *yelling*", I yell back at her.

My green dream is a patron to my deranged sleep. My fear for dinosaurs has grown 10 times from the last two months, since I last met him.

I don't need him in my life. He used me. He desolated me. I hate him.

Moving on in life is the hardest part of ending a part of your life. Beginning from the beginning. You know you have lost some part of yourself, still you are standing, confronting the cruel reality. The reality that kicks you on your bums again and again, and still the only options you are left with are to either lay down and act like a zombie, or stand up again in a hope to kick the bums of your life.

Sometimes I still feel him besides me. Holding my hands. Staring in my eyes saying, 'I love you'. I have nightmares where my ears would hallucinate these three whispered words. Where the echo of my thoughts haunt me. Where his existence in my past belongs to his absence in my future. I could move on, only if I would want to move on from him.

"Rachel!"

"I'm coming mom. Just a sec", I forgot it was her moving day. Well, temporary moving day. My bare feet reach out for their ardor, white fluffy slippers gifted by my Indian childhood friend. I used to envy him for his naturally tanned skin.

"Say hi to Nipun for me", I say as my mother releases me from her embrace.

"Of course darling! You take care of yourself, and your Lindsey. Don't party around all the time. Don't bring your boyfriend when I am gone", she winks at me.

"Mom, I don't *have* a boyfriend.*"

"Then make one! Remember darling, I trust you. I know you won't choose a person who would break your heart."

What if someone has already broken me mom?

"On a serious note, stay away from basketball players and don't underestimate or trust any stranger. Okay?", she adds. She has always been over-protective, especially when it comes to the basketball players. I have asked her the reason a million times, but every time I get the same reply, 'Just trust me, darling! I want you to be safe.'

I nod.

Her golden hair is peeking from the cab window, the car engine revs, bestowing me for a good lonely time. I used to live in my own apartment about 10 blocks from here, until it was burnt by my best friend - my Canadian roommate. Querie was my neighbor since I moved to California from India. She became my best friend a day after my moving day.

I giggle at the thought and go to my solitary phase. It was March end and I was 9 years old when I first saw that red-headed girl living across the street. It was *not* the love at first sight. It was more of an envy from her mischievous eyes.

The next day she came to me with a bucket of red paint and said that that was blood. I took the bucket and colored her red from the same bucket by twisting it on her head, expecting her to cry and never revert in my life. Since life is full of unexpected adventures, she laughed and hugged me and said, 'Now we both are wrapped in the color of love and war', and we have been best friends since then.

Childhood is enigmatic. We find happiness in everything. I didn't give a single thought on the wastage of blood, I know now that it was red paint and she came to scare me with her another mischievous uncertainty, and I spilled all of it just to vex her out of my life and we ended up as mischievous best buddies for our lifetime.

When I think of childhood, I think of eyes. Children's eyes are the most innocent and honest scene of the nature. You cannot hate them, you always love them no matter how big a mistake they do. No matter how many times they will desolate you, you will still love them. But with adults, there is a whole new cruel world waiting to tear you apart, making you beg for mercy in the devil's phase.

I spread my arms to let Lindsey's warmth surround me. My most faithful friend, my Beagle. She is now 4 years old. I love playing with her big ears. Tickling on the area between her neck and forelegs makes her involuntarily scratch herself. Her brown fur, corrupted by black and white patches makes her even more adorable. I blow on her face and she kisses me on my lips, well, not exactly kiss. Her saliva floats in the air like some poison waiting for its host.

"l love you the most Lindsey", I stretch her naughty body on my stomach with her mouth on my breasts, and sleep with her on my black couch, hoping not to acquaint with my green dream again.

3.

Love. Betrayal. Commitment.

The order in which my life went from the color of harmony to the color of destruction. My love betrayed me and I committed myself to my career.

I go to my room and reach my muffled life, expressed into the letters colored in blue, with the handwriting of my feelings. My diary is as new as it is old. I stopped putting my days into words since he betrayed me. Its brown colored cover is pulling me into my past, where I decided to let go of everything.

I open the first page.

Continued…

2013

Next page.

January 7,2013

Today Nipun showed a picture of his new girlfriend. She was good. But very fat.

My dad has delayed his return again, and I don't want to accept how much I miss him.

My mom was crying again. I don't understand her reasons of sobbing many a times.

Today Querie and I were suspended from the school. AGAIN. This time it wasn't even our mistake. Miss Queen seduced a student for the first base. We were just helping Jay from falling into her trap. Guess, we earned the vacations.

Next page.

January 12, 2013

Lesson learned today:

Do not destroy any relation by considering just its negative part.

Many a times a relationship breaks when you only see its negative part. When your friend does something negative, you keep that in mind and react just on that basis. At that time, recall your good times with him/her and ask yourself, "Is he/she worth leaving?" and then act on the basis of your answer.

Relationships are precious. Don't let them walk away from you so easily.

January 20, 2013

Querie and I were suspended. Yet again. Well, this time it was our fault. We introduced Miss Queen's undergarments with some bugs. Big bugs. And she caught us in her apartment's front camera. Better luck next time!

Nipun got dumped today, by his FAT girlfriend. I consoled him by saying that he was lucky to break away from that fat lady. When I acquainted him with the facts of making love with a fat lady, he felt much better, and thanked me.

I had a long talk with my father. He seemed frustrated about India. Said he will be back as soon as his bastard boss was done with his work. I can't fathom how much my mother would have been missing him.

February 3, 2013

Looking out the window

I feel something

My heartbeats

It is missing something

Rhythm of life

Its emptiness is calling me

Calling the love in me

I am looking for love

My one true love

Turn. Turn. Turn.

After flipping about half the diary, my love life began.

February 8, 2014

I found my new crush today. Mr. John Wright. My new arts teacher. He is definitely the right guy for me. And yeah,

Querie also has a crush on him. So we made a pact today: The one whose prom partner will be a ruin at the end of our prom night can have Mr. 'Sweet' John. We are going to dump our prom partners. Hehahaha.

My father is still living at Nipun's place.

I haven't had a talk with Nipun. Don't know what's wrong with him. It's going to be a fortnight today.

February 15, 2014

I got in touch with Nipun after a long time. He was having a bad time coz of the death of his grandmother. I soothed him for 3 hours or so. Completely lost track of time.

Erik Heartz. I don't know who chose this awkward name. But he is the one for me. The one whom I am going to dump like a reckless garbage on my prom night. It's going to be fun.

Mr. 'Sweet' John took his shirt off in front of the whole class today. Well, Querie and I got suspended for adding totally HARMLESS beetles in his handsome chest. Still, it was worth the punishment.

February 17, 2014

Our mission 'Earn John' has begun. I followed Erik to the mall today. And Qeurie followed her bait named James. Erik was alone, and that was my best chance to wrap him up in my web of love. I reached a shop, where he wanted to buy his prom dress, I eavesdropped. He was looking for the perfect suit, and I was looking for an exposing evening gown. I didn't find a gown, but I chose a whore dress. I took a transparent crochet crop top, black in color, and a super mini skirt, leather black. I used the trial room for exposing my sexiness. He was trying his gentleman-ness besides mine. I waited for him to move out of the protection holding my bait. As he did so, I slipped myself into his… well, I slipped on the floor, which I intended not to do, but fell in his warm arms. And when he helped me, I made him fall on me. My peeking breasts were wanting his attention, were touching his black velvety suit.

4.

Living in the memories is all I have got at present. I am in love with a wonderful person, and that person has left me for no reason. So I go back in my mind, to the day when we first met and lived *our* time.

My breasts were peeking out for his attention in the changing room, and his eyes were fixed on mine. *Why is he looking in my eyes?* I thought he would ogle at my breasts, and then I would entrap him in my bewitchery. I was below him, all messed up, well, intentionally messed up. He was blushing. I thought he was a playboy, but playboys don't blush, do they?

His eyes were green. Intense green. With a touch of hazel. He was looking in my eyes. My stomach started feeling that odd crush-like feeling. *I am going to dump him. Use him, and dump him. I am not going to fall for him.*

"I am so sorry… I… didn't see you there. I am astonished of how can I not observe such a handsome face", I flaunted, and he started raising himself from me. He stood and offered me his hand for support.

"No, the fault is mine, beautiful. I should have been more careful", I accepted his support, without making him fall on me again.

"What kind of dress are you looking for?", he asked me without ogling my breasts. *Why is he doing this? Does he know what kind of a person I am? Is he playing with my mind? He definitely is!*

"I am looking for a prom dress. What are you looking for?", *all I am interested is in using you sucker.*

"And who is your lucky partner?", he was acting sweet.

"Well, I am in search of one. I hope I get a guy like you", as I said, the other guy with the eye liner ogles my peeking body parts, and I give him a look of 'go to hell'. I fixed my eyes on Erik, and lowered the waist of my skirt a little bit to make him fall for me.

"You know, I know!", he said.

He knows??

"You know *what?*", my eyes widened like a full moon peeking in the empty world of souls.

"That you are trying to fool me with your looks to make me come to the prom with you", he smirked at my reaction.

I sigh. *Thank Jesus.*

"I have been observing you since we were kids. You are a girl with a pure heart, and I would love to come with you to the prom", he cut my silence.

Oh no! I trapped a good guy! Now what?

"Do you not want me to be your prom partner?", he added to my blank expression.

"Oh no, I would love to", I gave a big smile. I didn't know whether that smile was fake or real, but I was starting to like this guy.

5.

I told Nipun about Erik. Maybe I had found my love. Maybe I would lose my bet with Querie.

I talked to Erik for an hour or so today. He cares for me. But I don't understand why does he care for me so much? I don't even show him the real me.

I am all messed up in myself. My father is always the one who resolves me, and he is not anywhere near me, so I blurted out my babelism to Nipun. He listened to me so attentively, as if he was listening about football. He told me to write all my problems in a piece of paper, until I feel relaxed and then tear that paper into pathetic marooned pieces. And so I did, and it made me feel way better.

6.

I remember talking to Erik, meeting him, laughing at his jokes, being myself with him. I remember the smell of his breathe, the taste of his kiss, the night before the prom, and the prom day when everything turned to black from green. He desolated me when my mind changed from ruining him to marrying him. I fell in love with him, so I decided to lose my 'Sweet John's' bet, but Erik ruined me in return.

I lost myself to him the night before the prom night, when I gave everything of mine to him. I was living with Querie in our apartment, and I had had a fight with her. She went to her boyfriend, so I called up mine.

He was standing in my room, tasting my lips with his naked mouth. I held to him even stronger when he pushed me on my bed. Touched my belly with his cold hands. I shivered and wrapped myself in his ardor. His stomach was my armor. He slipped his finger below my belly-button, touching my solitary part, then opened the button of my jeans. I slipped my hands into his pants and made him want me even more. We moved towards the end of the bed, moving back and forth in each other's arms. He kissed my breasts, while I struggled with my subconscious mind. I listened to his heartbeats, while he kissed my forehead. We rolled over each other, caressing each other's souls. His body was cold, and his breathe was addictive to me. I looked at him, wanting to kiss him more. He stared at me, wanting to fill me up. We were made for each other. We were together, it's the miracle of life. Love was my life and I would always be there for my life, living to love.

I was sleeping on his inflating and deflating lungs. His heartbeats were as clear and as lovable as if he was born to be my hero of love.

"Wake up sleeping beauty", an unexpected voice welcomed me in the morning. The morning of the prom day.

"Querie?", I pulled myself from my last night's glory, to find myself naked on the bed, alone. I covered my body with my blanket and sat up, "Where is Erik?"

"How would *I* know that?", she rolled her eyes and a shock of abandonment swept through me. *No, he can't do that. He is different. He would have gone for some work, not wanting to disturb me.*

"I am sorry for snapping at you, Raech. I was disturbed, and James made it worse by…",Querie was apologizing for her rudeness, but I was lost in my thoughts.

I looked around my bed to find any sign of his belongings. His watch was lying on the bed-side table, shining his return to me. *He is definitely coming back today.He won't leave me alone on my prom night. My bet ended up finding my true love. I know he is my one true love.*

It was the night of my prom.

He promised me he would pick me up at 7. He can't break his promise. He will come for me. I was sitting on the stairs of my apartment, watching people passing by in front of me, while I was searching for just one face. A face having hazel green eyes, dark hair, and the lips with my essence. Every voice seemed his. Every call waited for his name.

"Where are you?", my heart ache gave its way to these words of whisper.

"Rachel?", I turned back to see Querie dressed up in blue sheath-shaped evening gown, "Where is Erik?"

"On his way", my heart knew it was true, but my mind begged for his return.

"Should I stay with you?", his bait was waiting for her in his Ford.

"Absolutely not! He will be here in no time. You go and have your time", I gave her a big fake smile, and looked at the passing time in his desolated wrist watch.

"I can see something's wrong Raech. Call me if you need something. Alright?"

I nodded and she went away.

I was sitting in my black Mermaid style evening gown, rather in my strapless crochet and my prostitute-attire, as I imagined my prom night once. I giggled and cried.

One hour.

Two hours.

Three hours.

I went in my room, got out of my dress, burned it and watched myself naked, shining in the color of flames in the mirror. *He dumped me.*

"Why did you do that?", I shouted with all my energy, "Come in front of me. Answer me! Why did you do this to me?"

I cried until all my tear glands dried up. Until it was four hours after midnight. Until my body couldn't feel anything. Until even the cold wind couldn't hurt my bare body. Until I decided to commit my life to my career.

7.

Since the day he desolated me, I am having the same green terrifying dream every other night of my life. First, I thought that my green dream is beckoning me to save the nature Earth, but I don't know why it would show my worst fear killing me.

Dinosaurs are my only fear in front of whom I can shit my pants. It is my fear that can haunt me even in my most judicious days, and this fear has been killing me for 2 months every other night in my dreams.

I turn the pages of my diary to the days when I used to drown myself in my own self.

May 13, 2014

You are like me

The one who could trust

The one who could be loved

You will always stay in my heart

You will always stay my heart

Be with me

In the world of cruelty

Never leave me

For this is me

Look into my eyes

Look into your soul

It is the one thing

I have always wanted

It is you

And it is us

May 24, 2014

I called him

He didn't listen

I called him again

But received only silence

Silence of my death

Death of my love

Love which resided in my heart once

Has been lost in this world

World of cruelty

And world of abandonment

Leaving me alone

Always alone

May 29, 2014

I wanted you

I needed you

I had you

I lost you

You were my heart

You were my soul

Don't leave me

Don't let go of me

I will be here only

Waiting for you

Waiting for the sun

In the darkness of my grimness

I will be waiting

Till I die

It's all blank afterwards. There was nothing for me to write. No sorrow. No happiness to share. Only emptiness. I decided to let go of him. I decided to throw him out of my life, and the only thing to write for me was nothing.

8.

The person I needed the most was myself, since I forgot who I really was, how I used to enjoy every moment of my life, how I used to invent ideas to plan another prank.

Querie helped to pull me out of my break-up phase, and I helped myself pull from my own bootstraps.

Since Querie and I were the artistic minds, we decided to choose arts in our further studies. We both went into wildlife painting and fortunately got the same college. Before, I used to put myself into words in my diary, and now, I am a brush of some width of existence, expressing myself into the colors of life, or you can say, finding *my* colors of life.

I still talk to Nipun every day. He keeps me away from my emptiness, but the hole has already found its home in my heart. That hole cannot be filled with anything else but true love.

I am filling colors in a blank canvas, trying to pet my own cub, filled with orange and black stripes, when I see a worried lady with a knee-length pencil skirt and a formal shirt searching for someone. Her outer appearance is sophisticated, while her face shows her concern for someone. She is Erik's mother. *What, in the world, is she doing here?* She is searching in different classrooms. *I have never seen Erik around here. Then who is she searching for?*

She comes to my class and asks my mentor, "Is Rachel Cox here?"

My heartbeats start racing in synchronization with my mind. *What the hell?* I get goose bumps all over my body. I can see my hands shaking and my tiger cub waving its way on the canvas. Querie turns her head to me with an askance look. I shrug and get trapped in my past when Erik's mother finds me.

"Rachel! Can I talk to you in private?", she seems really concerned about something. *Is Erik alright? Please tell me it's not about him. Jesus, please keep him alright.*

I gulp all my nervous nail-biting habit and try walking with her without wobbling. We reach the other corridor of the classes. There is just a peon, mopping the tiles, a strained lady and a nerve-racked student. She stops, turns towards me, and says, "I have been looking for you in the whole world".

You should have gone to my home, and you would have found me. I mock myself but don't feel like giggling on my own joke.

She continues, "Have you seen Erik?"

"What?", my eyeballs can jump out of my eyes, and my mouth stays wide open, giving invitation to the nearby houseflies.

She seems blank, out of answers, out of any more questions.

"What has happened to him? Is he alright?", my mouth automatically confronts to my heart.

She replies, disappointed, "Yes, yes, he is totally fine. Just searching for him", she murmurs and finds her way to the exit while murmuring to herself.

I know something's wrong. I have to know what's wrong.

9.

I am standing in front of his house. Red door is waiting for his return. He is definitely not at home. *Where are you Erik?* I see his mother in his room. This is not a good time to trespass his room.

I decide to trespass later and walk to my home, praying for his well-being and feeling guilty for my arrogance. *What if something has happened to him? What if he was going to come at the prom, and something unfortunate happened?*

I lie on my bed, hugging his photo on my mobile phone. The photo that I snapped the night before prom night.

He was kissing my stomach, making me feel nauseated and I had drank too much alcohol to make him feel the same way. I got impish and was playing with his hair, he started to lower down his face and I started nudging him on his head. His phone rang and he stopped, making me hang in that phase of desperation. I snatched his phone, the call went into voicemail, I kissed him wildly and took his intoxicated snapshot from his phone, his eyes were red, trying to give their way for my sight, and only my sight. He was not drunk, but he was in state of inebriety of love, true love for me.

I start weeping in his remembrance, for the lost time, that can't come back to me the same way. The days that went by so fast, but seem now, so slow. I start crying in vain, with an aching heart, wanting my heart to come out of me forever, and stop hurting me. I whisper his name again and again, wanting him to hug me and apologize for his mistakes, and assure me never to leave me again. I wish him to be here with me, lying in my bed, with my head on his chest, counting his heartbeats and making it my lullaby. The tears fall on my pillow, making it wet and calling me into my world of dreams.

10.

"Help me Rachel. I am sorry for everything you had to face because of me. I am responsible for every drop of tear that fell from your longing eyes. I would have come if I could have come. I would have hugged you, if I could have escaped from this trap. Save me from myself. Save me from this prison with no exit", Erik's gloomy voice echoes all over my green house. I search for him in all the green rooms, on the green road and reach his green house without finding a soul except my craving one.

I find myself standing at the same place where my fear killed me in my last dream and I fight for an escape when his voice continues, "Rachel, you are the only hope left for me. Go to my room, find a green capsule kept in the first drawer of my study table, intake it and sleep in my room. You will find all the answers to my desolation. Always in love with you".

Gone! His voice. Green dream. It's all gone, leaving me feeling empty in this colorful world. My eyes are wet, searching for the answers to my pandemonium. I look at my black watch, left alone like me by Erik. He told me that it was his grandmother's last gift to him, and so I loved it like it contains Erik's heart and I am its guardian. It tells me it's 11.55 at night, and this is the right time for me to enter in his room and reveal his secrets.

I sneak out of my house, walk to his house following the full moon, climb through the pipeline to his room and strike myself with the flood of emotions. I switch on the lights to find that his room is clean, so clean that I can see my own reflection from the wooden furniture. The cleanliness is provoking me to mess up his room, but I fathom this is not the right time for my distractions, it's time to get back with Erik and get answers for my fumbled mind.

I reach his study table. I see his photo frame, in which he is wearing a yellow T-shirt with my photo of pouting my mouth printed on it. I had no idea that he had done such a thing. *Was he going to gift this to me?*

I open the first drawer of his study table. A green capsule is lying on its own, waiting for its rightful owner to come and own it. I have seen this capsule before. *Oh my god! It is the same pill that I spat on the paw of the dinosaur, and the dinosaur's paw burst into flames bringing me to my death bed in my green dreams.*

My hands start shaking. *What is this? Some kind of a joke? How can this be real?*

I don't understand what to do next. *I have to find Erik. I have to be strong and follow his voice. I have to find the hanging answers to my perplexed situation.*

Without giving way to any other thought of fear, I took that pill in my dry mouth and gulped it at once.

He told me to sleep on his bed after taking the pill, and so I do.

I take his photo frame and lay on his bed keeping his photo close to my heart. This time I am not going to cry, because I know that I am going to him. I am unaware of my conveyance towards him, but all I know is I am going back to him and I am not going to lose him this time.

I start feeling dizzy and go into the world of my subconscious mind.

The last thing I remember of the real world is a heavy evil voice, "The game begins!"

11.

I can't open up my eyes, it's stuck with gluey morsel. I feel myself lying on the grass, in the open, where blowing wind is welcoming me into the unknown and perilous conveyance.

"Save me", Erik's voice calls to me.

I smash open the doors of my eyeballs. He is nowhere near me. I try to call him, tell him that I need him, but the only sound I can hear is of growling.

'Woof woof! Woooooo… wooooo", *what the hell is happening? Why can't I talk?*

It's my voice. I am growling and howling. I am still lying on the ground. Now I can see my legs, my four legs, in front of me, resting on the same ground, attached to my hairy brown body.

I am dumb-struck. *I am definitely dreaming.*

I get up on my four legs to scrutinize my new dream world around me. It is a forest. I can hear the voice of wind, communicating through the leaves, whispering about my love for Erik, beckoning me to wrap myself in his arms, begging me to save his life.

I don't know what animal I am, but I am definite that I am dreaming, and that to apart from my usual green dream.

Am I that *attached to animals that I* always *dream of them?* This time I have crossed the limit by *becoming* one!

There is no way to find out my breed of animal. I would need a mirror to do that.

My ears alert my other senses by reacting to the sound of footsteps. I am loving my new enhanced senses. The fallen leaves wrestle with the human's footsteps as a human approaches me.

Erik would have sent her to help me reach him. Her silhouette turns into opaque structure of a perfectly made divine angel. But… *why is she naked?*

Her figure is perfect. Her hair is golden. Her skin is white. She is untouched and pure having the forge of a newly-born baby, shining under the blessings of sun and descended on the Earth through the bare hands of God.

I realize that I am sitting on my hind legs, wagging my tail in the admiration of her beauty. She is standing an inch away from me, naked from body and soul. She sits on her knees, stares me in my eyes, and I see her consummate brown eyes. She hugs me, wrapping my fluffy neck in her bare hands and her breasts giving my flossy chest to feel the coolness of her outer skin.

She whispers in my ears, "Lindsey!"

Lindsey? This name sounds so familiar. Lindsey…? Oh my God! Lindsey!? As in she is my bitch, Lindsey?

I tilt my head in response. I want to communicate with my Lindsey. What is happening? This is my weirdest dream ever. I want to talk.

She parts me away from her, looks into my eyes and says, "Go inside that farmhouse", pointing towards an abandoned old house that has a smelly mouth and unbathed edifice.

Her hair smells like sweet lavender, blowing towards me, while she says, "Go!"

12.

I step on the wooden floor, my paws making negligible noise, but dead leaves are provoking them to emanate my presence.

There is a well, opened for me to drown in my past. I can see my past coming alive. I can see the flames burning in my head and taking me to the vivid farmhouse, awaiting my return to the well.

I used that well to stir my consciousness when Nipun used to tease me by painting my face with mud and used to say, "Now we match each other's complexion".

I was standing where I am standing right now, and saved him from jumping from that same well which turned to be an evil escape for his mother when she sacrificed her life to that well and Nipun was about to imitate her mistake.

"No Sonu! Stop!", I shouted while he was standing at the edge of that well and his life. He turned towards me, ran and hugged me. He cried till the moon did farewell and sun gave its way to the new beginning.

I saved his life that night. Fate didn't let me lose my friend.

It is the same farmhouse where I -am standing, it is the same well which snatched away Nipun's happiness in just a moment, and held Nipun in his arms, calling him in it.

Why am I back to this place? I have never thought or dreamt about this well since I was 15 years old. I moved on and stopped giving my time to the conce*-pt of death or reality.

The vivid past blackens and the farmhouse becomes sick with emptiness and eerie memories.

"Welcome to our world, Rachel", my hairy ears are craving for Erik's voice, and all I get is a black man with white hair and a broken voice. For a moment, I imagined him as *Morgan Freeman.*

He is wearing a florescent blue pair of pants and a jacket, with a black shirt, making his appearance a moving joke for me.

"Whose wedding are you coming from, old idiosyncratic black man?", I mock him forgetting all about my ominous surroundings.

Wait a sec! I just talked!

"Yeah, you can talk when you are with me, no matter who or what you will be", he replies as if he can read my thoughts.

"Where is Erik?"

"Stuck on the last level."

"Last level? Last level of *what*?"

His eyes are black and as inhumane as they can be. I am beginning to become afraid of those eyes staring at me from above, an imbecile human being.

"Last level of Gablet."

"Now what in the world is this Gablet?"

"It's a game. You are on its first level at present. You will be given a task in every level. You can move onto the next level only if the given task is completed", he is addressing me as if he is standing in front of a myriad audience.

"Am I not dreaming?"

"You are! Gablet is the game of dreams. The difference between Gablet and a normal dream is that the creatures, including you, dying in this world of dreams will lose their mental stability in the real world."

My eyes go down to my feet, not scrutinizing the dirt stuck on my hairy paws, but trying to adapt to the words that touched my new senses.

If Erik dies here, he will die in real life, I mean, he will be alive, but dead from inside. I need to reach him fast.

I deter to my emotions by responding him with, "What is my task?"

He points towards the well. My eyes follow to the floating black hole above the well, and again towards the empty space where the old man existed a second ago, vanishing into vapors, leaving me to struggle between my past and future.

I walk towards the well, finding a bubble, the phantom flamboyant black hole lying above the emptiness of Nipun's mother's soul.

I can see my reflection through that bubble. A large brown creature with a bulk of hair, waving with the slow-moving wind. My ears held up straight with my huge scary face. My muzzles sheltering with temporary home to the dirt particles. I am a wolf, or some kind of a dog.

I rustle some more leaves to be able to read my first step to reaching Erik. It reads, 'Kill Lyndsey'.

13.

It was 8 years later from the death of Nipun's mother when he found out why she died. He used to cry every day after her death, cursing himself for not understanding the mental disturbance of his mother. He was just 5 years old, but he understood well that she killed herself, and I knew that it was not his fault. I was the only friend he had at that time. We used to meet every day when he would lie on my laps and cry about his misfortune.

"Why did she leave me, Rachel? Am I that bad? Did I... frustrate her by my talks? Did I...", he would break into inconsolable cries and I would cry with him.

I left India to settle in California when we were 9, and I used to visit India with my father every half yearly.

It was cold in Shimla, India, when I had searched every corner of Nipun's house for him, but couldn't find any sign of him. I walked towards his farmhouse to find him wrapped in himself. His head was buried under his shin, his legs were drawn towards his hips and he was shivering and sobbing intermittently.

He was back to back with a long tree trunk lying on the ground. I caressed his hair, he wiped his tears while his head was still burrowed under his own warmth, and raised his head to search for the person who has found him.

"What happened? Tell me", my voice softened like a melody.

His glassy black eyes were saying so much, while his lips were moving just to inhale and sob.

I removed his hands from his own shell, held it with both of my hands and asked, "What happened?"

He hugged me tightly and started crying with all his energy left. After giving out all his negative emotions, he replied, "My mother... was pregnant... with another child... but of someone else's... and she jumped... as a result of fear of our society", his sobs again turned into wails.

He was unknown of his mother's reason of death all those years. He was unknown of the one truth that he was searching in so many past endeavors.

"Raech... I should have done something... I should have... stopped her...", his deep black eyes were fixed on mine. Both of us were crying.

"It wasn't your fault, Sonu. It is this society. It is this cruel world which is unfair and brutal to good people. Good people *always* suffer, because this universe needs the *best* one to survive its miracles."

14.

I am on four legs. Lindsey is sitting naked, with the same posture as I found Nipun in, back to back with the tree log, which gave support to Nipun once.

What will I do now? Kill her? Kill my angel?

I raised her, and now I have to kill her? Just to save Erik? I can't be this cruel. I can't kill her.

But what about Erik? I can't let him die in this...

What is this? What is... what did he say? Gab... I don't even remember its name.

Erik, I need you. I need you to come and tell me what to do. Please come!

I am howling. Lindsey turns her green eyes from the gossiping trees to a four-legged creature. This is the right opportunity to grab her neck and pull away a part of her from my pointed killer canines.

What am I thinking? I can't kill her. I love her.

She is staring at me, nothing to speak of, no innocent questions to ask about. *Has she sensed that I am about to kill her?*

I am at a war with myself. What should I choose? My love is at stake. While on the other side, I have been parenting my Lyndsey since she was just 2 months old. She was and always have been my companion, even when the whole world left me alone, to grieve and to laugh.

I remember the day when I found her in the pet shop, gazing me with admiration, with her inculpable shiny eyes, so large and so enchanting. How can I even think of hurting her?

My heart is triumphant, at last. *Who am I kidding? I can't kill her. She's my angel. I would rather die saving her. I need to find another way for getting out of my dream and saving Erik.*

Before becoming a dog, I used to talk and fight and argue with myself, and now I am a soliloquizing dog.

While I am circumvolving between Lindsey and Erik, my painting of orange skin with black stripes came alive, walking with stealth, an adult tiger who is waiting for the right time to have supper that contains golden hair and soft velvety skin. I can see the tiger crawling towards Lindsey, aiming for her neck, Lindsey's neck being the eye of the bird for *Arjuna*.

My heart starts beating faster and louder. The stripes on the twilight expanse has ambushed approximately 50 meters away from my bitch. Her innocent green eyes were waiting for me to provide succorance to her purity.

The tiger is reducing the distance between itself and Lindsey. I am the third vertex of the sanguinary triangle, with other two vertexes to be the tiger and Lindsey, simultaneously.

My pace is in twain with my heartbeats and with tiger's ravenous stomach. Within seconds, the beast is just 10 meters away from the beauty, while the brown-colored beast is 5 meters away.

My subconscious mind starts dominating and takes control of my hairy paws.

The tiger soars to bite the neck out of Lindsey, I alight to grab the tiger. My mind knows that this is not the case of volition I should have chosen, but I love Lindsey and I won't lose her just because I welcomed trouble in my life.

The tiger's eyes are glued on Lindsey, while I make it shift its eyes to me, both tiger and I in the air, Lindsey's facial expression turning from jolly to fear, her eyes turning from relaxed to mutiny. I grab the tiger's leg, throw it on the ground, rolling one above other, bathing with the dirt, when suddenly we come to a halt. A big striped cat is above a four-legged brown wild dog. *I cannot overpower him.* He roars, his teeth beckoning my death. *I am sorry Erik.*

It is my first near-death experience. Everything slows down to let me observe with serenity. I feel as if I have completed my present life, it's time to let go of my soul and scrutinize the reason of my living. I can feel my heartbeats matching the speed of light. I can feel his claws clutching me on my deathbed. I can feel his carnassial teeth approaching my neck, ready to shear it apart. His breath touching my whiskers.

"I love you", Erik's voice whispers in my dog ears. The voices of my panting, tiger's growling, my whining, Lindsey's crying, leaves' wrestling, trees' gossiping, all numbs and I can feel Erik's lips touching my cheek, his humanly touch to my humanly desperate skin, wanting him above and inside me.

The tiger vanishes, Erik's touch vanishes, an aghast Lindsey vanishes, the farmhouse vanishes, the supportive tree log vanishes, the forest vanishes, and I welcome blackness into my sight and my soul.

15.

"Wake up, sleepy head", it is not Erik's amorous voice that I have been longing for a century, but it is an alien-looking history teacher.

I raise my head, my hands folded on the table, my saliva on my sleeves, my hair all messed up, and my eyes half-closed. Mr. Bottleneck is standing in front of me, his eyes fixed on my sleepy eyes. His surname suits him well. He is a fat-thin guy. I don't know how to describe him. He is fat below his breasts and thin above his chest. His abdomen's fat is as large as a whole whale residing in it, while his face is no thinner than an ant's.

Well, I am exaggerating, but you get the big picture.

He is wearing a pair of round Harry Potter spectacles below his invisible eyebrows and blonde hair.

"You think teaching sloths is fun? You can have your bed there", he is pointing towards the vicinity near the window to my left where six large white tiles have nothing but dust listening to Mr. Bottleneck's history and not the world's history, "and cuddle up to your dreamboy", he mimics cuddling from his hands.

After that sentence, all my conscious mind could capture was, "blah… blah… blah…", something about a donkey, "blah… blah… blah… Get out of my class".

I am glad I heard the last line distinctly.

I does as he says, thrive myself up from my chair, help my legs move outside the class and upstairs towards the roof. There is a notice board hanging on the wall before the entrance of the roof, displaying the paintings from lower to higher graded students.

One painting catches my eyes. It has a 3D effect where a horse is running on a racing track and there is a hole in front of the horse. That hole seems like a tornado. That hole can send the horse to another dimension. Or, that hole can be the end of his life. The horse is covered with a check-rein and blinkers, which prevents him from measuring his path with his full senses. He will fall into that hole, the hole made by the mean world, the abyss of sins of human world which is destroying not just their lives, but the lives of everyone else living around them.

The name of the artist is Lolita, written in calligraphy in the right bottom corner of the painting.

Every drawing has its own story, it all depends on the observer and his perceptions. The painting will show the observer the world that he wants to see. It will reflect the image of his own life. Artists are the people who would give the world more than they take, they will show the world how they see it, and they live their lives with fire.

"I always know where to find you", Querie's aroused voice startles me, bringing me back to the matrix of reality.

"That Bottleneck is a pain-in-the-ass. He just keeps on babbling and he doesn't realize how much his students want to murder him…", she continues.

Murder! This word strikes me back to Gablet. To Erik.

"Where's Erik?", I cut the red-headed girl from chattering.

"I don't know. He is *your* brother, you should be the one tracing his roving", she prompts.

"My *brother*?", my pitch goes up, all confused.

"What has happened? Why are you crying?", her face turns blue.

I wipe my tears from my eyes. Erik is waiting for me to go and save him, and I *will* save him, I *need* to save him.

"I don't have a brother, Querie", as I say this, I get a zombie Querie. She doesn't react, she just stares at me in my eyes, as if she is going to fall in her bedlam.

"Say something", I am dying to know what's going on in her head.

She brings her hand on my forehead, predicting my body heat through her palm.

"What are you doing?", I snap at her as I lose my patience, "Tell me where Erik is?"

"Raech, should I call a doctor?", her expressions are singing like a nightingale, sweet and caring.

I turn backwards to the roof's balustrade and to the clear blue sky.

"Can you show me his photo?", I could barely hear my own voice, but Querie heard and takes out her mobile from her left pocket of her pencil-fit low-waist jeans.

"Internet makes available everything nowadays", her eyes are fluttering with the browsing screens, "Here!", she stretches her hand to me to let me see his photo.

I take the mobile to look at the heart-skipping photo of Erik. He is standing on a beach, covering his lower-body with just a pair of boxers, the moonlight being his umbrella, protecting him from the ominous powers of the huge dark monster, and he is smiling at me revealing his innocence.

With a ring of bell, lunch break welcomes itself and my tears.

I give back her mobile phone to its rightful owner and run to the ground floor, to get lost in the grotesque crowd.

16.

I excuse myself from the world, emancipate from the battles inside my head. I walk along with the wind. The wind that is delivering me the sweet kisses to my cheeks by my love. Wind is the communicator of my feelings to Erik.

I am walking on the pavement, passing across the people with indiscernible faces, passing through the places with no names. My eyes fixed on my shoes, my hands under the pocket of my jacket, and my mind lost in my train of thoughts.

The sun is giving its throne to the moon, and I to my epiphanies.

I have been so wrapped up in my new found love that I forgot about my mother visiting my father in India. I want to talk to her and ask her whether father would be able to come home at last, whether the problem has been solved.

Heart is a strange organ. It can drown your mind in it, giving it no chance of considering anything else.

I ramble on with the wind, to find myself standing in front of a horse barn that my father owned in India.

Shimla city comes in the Northern India, the capital city of Himachal Pradesh. This city of hills was my childhood home. The place where I lived my first

8 and half years. The place where I met my best friend, Nipun. The place where I found my true self. Yet, how we, Americans, started living in India is still anonymous to me.

Getting one's own place in Shimla is as difficult as finding luxury in a dense forest of South Africa. Nipun's father helped my father to settle there.

"Sam", I run towards my escape from the cruelty and reality. I hug him. His heartbeats are just the same when I last saw him a year ago. When I saw him dying in front of my eyes. When I wept all over him when he was buried under the ground. When Nipun held me from falling to the ground.

Sam is my Peruvian Paso, my black beauty, my colt, or I should say, he was. He took his last breathe on the 3th of June the previous year.

His hair is reflecting the moonlight, bathing him from the open window, which is sheltering a spider to my right. He neighs and hugs me back.

"I missed you, kido", I laugh and cry at the same time and he exhales, making my hair tangle with his breathe. His smell is touching my soul making me fall in love with him, again.

His left hind leg knuckle is whining in my ears to medicate it. I find a first aid box near the window, I pick it up, and treat him, and now, not even God can take him away from me. This has happened in my dreams uncountable times, and at present, I am living in one of those times.

A year ago when I visited India, his left hind leg knuckle infected his whole leg and it was too late to treat him, and he died, in front of my blurry wet eyes.

For now, I want to spend all my time with him. His colt-tail is wagging and his happiness is soaring as much as I fonder him. I find a chair near the window, pull it and sit next to him, hugging him.

I know I am still in that game, and the real Sam is buried under the farmhouse in India in the real world, and his soul transferred to some other cheerful horse, but I needed him and here he is, needing me. The people who can recognize the value of animals, can feel the warmth of being around them. Animals love you more than you would know, they adore you more than anyone else would in the world, they need you more than you think you need them, they bring you joy no matter how low you feel, and they make you feel the most special person one can be in the whole universe.

We are not heartless, or Hitler; animals feel the way you feel, they have their own soul, including the small insects that you would be ignoring in everyday life. Humans should respect every creature's feelings, and then only the world can become a better place.

When I was young, I used to talk to Sam for hours, about my Indian friends, my mother's mood swings, Nipun's frolics, and my other innocent doll-issues.

"Why do I have to wait so long for Erik, Sam? Why can't I just escape this game and meet him?", my childhood memories revive.

I close my eyes and let my senses feel myself. Sam's breathing, my breathing, the tangling of his mane, my breathing, and then, silence.

I sit with Sam with my numbness till I realize that it's past 11' o clock at night. I am reluctant to leave Sam again, I am afraid of losing him, but I need to move on, find Erik, save him and myself, and get in the real world with him.

I decide against my volition and stay with Sam. I may never see him again, never feel his silky hair, and never be able to talk to my black beauty. I decide to spend my night in his loving smell and return back to the game in the coming morning.

I hear my stomach growling and wish I had *two jumbo cheese pizzas without vegetables, and… with extra cheese.*

My wish comes true. There are two jumbo cheese pizzas on my right side, the side where the window is adjoining the outer dream world to my Sam. I pick it up and it has extra cheese and no vegetables.

17.

I open my eyes and it's dark. My head's on a pillow and my body lying on a soft bed. I jerk my torso up to a sitting posture.

"Where am I?", I say loudly and the darkness turns into man-made light. I turn my face to see bewildered Querie.

"Bad dream?", she asks as she scrutinizes the sweat on my head and the scratches on my hands and legs, "What happened to your hands? Mosquitoes? But there aren't any in my room!"

I look at my hands, and it's full of red marks and print of my nails. I try to remember where I have been. My home. Then Erik's home. Then... yeah... saving Erik. I crossed the first level without even completing its task. *How did I do that?*

I am interrupted by Querie, "What happened, Rachel? You seem so distracted since you attended Mr. Bottleneck's class."

This sentence takes me back to the memory of the painting of the horse drifting towards the abyss and *Sam*, and maybe I slept there, but how did I get here? And, what is here?

"Querie, don't think that I have lost my mind, but can you tell me where are we?"

She gazes me straight through my eyes for a moment and replies, "At my house".

I stare at her blankly, and she interprets that I have lost my mind and continues, "You asked me after the school if you could stay with me tonight, since you didn't want to go to your place, because of some clandestine reason."

I have no idea what she is talking about. I didn't ask her anything. "How did we get here?", I ask as I encounter short-term memory loss.

"With me, Raech. We walked together to my house after the school, then we watched movies on my laptop and ate jumbo-sized pizzas, and we laughed and had a pillow fight. Don't you remember any of these?"

She is concerned about my mental stability. I can understand what she would be feeling, but I have so much more to concern about right now.

"Maybe I need some sleep", I act unwell and lay back to bed without another word, my face away from worried Querie.

She switches off the night-lamp and without another word, lays back to bed as well.

I am sorry, Querie, for avoiding you and lying to you, but you are in my dream, and you won't remember any of this.

I try to dwell on the reason why did I say that I wanted to stay with her. Then I remember that Erik is

62

my younger brother in this level, or whatever this is, so I said it for good. I wouldn't be able to see my amorous love to stand in front of me and that to in the mask of my brother. I couldn't resist myself to not to kiss him and engrave him in myself.

It suddenly surrounds me that if Erik is in this level, then it might be the last level. I might have skipped all the other levels, and I need to save him in this level only.

I make sure that Querie is soundly asleep and make my way to the roof of Querie's house. I have been to her house a million times, but this house is different, this is someone else's house. *I need to get to the roof to find my house in front and to see if Erik's there or not.*

I manage to find the stairs to the roof and I reach to the top to find out that... I am in Canada.

18.

The moon is the usual bright and mesmerizing, but my view is more than 2,624 miles away from my previous location. I am somewhere in Toronto. I can tell this because I can see the 1,815.4 feet high CN Tower. I have heard a lot from Querie about its view from her home in her native country, and now, I am looking at the shining colors on it.

I might be in a dream, but it is more realistic than the reality. In this world, I see what is real to me, and not what people fake. In my world, there is innocence and honesty, unlike the outer world. I like this world, but there is a truth hidden behind the road to success, 'good and evil comes in parallel'. These opposite poles can change both the human paradigm and the universe, and that change can lead to progress and evolution, and that evolution might bring destruction, or something better.

I am staring at the moon, searching for my existence in the real world, thinking about the whereabouts of Erik, his lips, his smile, his smell, his taste.

A lightning strikes my senses, appearing physically at the center of the roof. I turn around and see that same ominous black flamboyant balloon, waiting for me in the center of the roof.

I go near it and read, 'Kill Querie's Shadow'.

"Querie's shadow?", I soliloquy, "How can anyone kill a shadow?". After dwelling on for a moment, "For killing any shadow, the body itself needs to be killed".

I become dumb-struck from my own theories. I turn back towards the moon, with the CN tower obstructing my view, I continue, "But after anybody's death, the shadow still remains with the dead body".

My theory brought me both relief and confusion.

"Should I bring light to the shadow? It will disappear then!", after another silent thinking, "But that won't be killing it, that would be just masking it."

The task seems encoded, and I can't think of any way to decode it. I turn towards the moon which has always supported me in my blue.

What is Querie's shadow? How can a shadow be killed?

What is this, Gablet? At least you could have cleared out your task.

Then I think, the gamer would be bored watching a monotonous play and would want me to turn his bore into merriment.

I struggle with myself, battle with the truth and false of my logics. My mind wavers from Querie to Erik to Shadow to Erik to Lindsey to Erik. I miss him. I wish he could be here, holding my hands, answering my flood of questions, solving my own rivals, but he is far away from me, waiting for me to save him, he needs me, and I will be there for him.

"KILL HER...", a croaking evil voice entraps me, strangling my neck with its hands.

I try to speak, to ask who it is and what it wants, but my throat is choking, my breathing becomes difficult. I try to shout, try to ask for help, try to call Querie, Erik, Nipun, my dad, or anybody who could come and save me from this cataclysm.

I turn around to the strangler, and it'sQuerie, but with some virtual make-up.

Her face is dark and her eyes hollow. It's her body, but not her soul. The person standing in front of me is dead from inside.

Suddenly she cringes back, afraid of something, her face becomes paler, eyes fixed on my neck. *What is she looking at?*She is walking backwards, away from me, her croak voice is now dispersing away from me. Her 'KILL HER' turns to 'NOOO'.

Why did she want to kill me?

I look at my neck, and I am wearing a chain, with the locket of Jesus' cross. *Why is she is afraid of that?*

I have watched enough movies to predict the behavior of an evil soul, or in other words, a ghost. What Querie did resembles the behavior of an evil lost soul.

I take out Erik's mobile from my pocket, and Google for the synonyms of Ghost.

Apparition

Appearance

Banshee

Daemon

Demon

Devil

Eidolon

Ethereal being

Haunt

Incorporeal being

Kelpie

Manes

Phantasm

Phantom

Revenant

Shade

Shadow

Shadow!

"Kill Querie's shadow, means, kill her ghost", I jump with triumph and fear. I continue, less to myself and more to Gablet, my hand pointing the door "That was Querie's *ghost?* I need to kill *that* thing?"

I didn't get any response, even though that was not rhetoric. So I ask again, "Gablet... Do you want me to kill *that?*"

All I can hear is the sound of wind, and my racing heartbeats. I close my eyes, take a long breathe and answer my own question, "I need to kill her ghost, but will it affect her in the real world?"

"No", it's cranky old man's voice.

I see upwards, to the sky, stark black, with just one source of light, one ray of hope, moon.

"Okay", I reply back and start following Querie's ghost.

She is afraid of my locket. That means, she cannot harm me as long as I have my cross.

I clutch my locket, the reason of my safety. I manage to find my way to Querie's room. She would be here somewhere, or I should say, *it* would be. That thing doesn't contain any soul. I can feel my steps slowing down, and my fear growing. I am afraid she would stab me from behind, so I keep looking at my back after every half a minute.

If I die here, I will lose Erik and my sanity. I can't die here.

I use my mobile phone as my torch and light my path, trying to find the soulless creature.

How will I kill that thing?

A girl is shouting, with the highest possible pitch. I turn backwards, there is no one. Before I could face the room, the creature jumps on me, hanging itself from my neck, and cringes back again. I guess it would have touched my locket. She wanted to take it off of me, but failed to do so.

I feel sad to see my best friend in this condition. I feel gloomy to call that red-hair pure hearted girl, a creature.

It's a dream, and a game. Let's end this and find Erik.

I remove my locket from my neck, grab the ghost from my other hand, and press the locket on its head, murmuring my favorite Bible verses, "For God has not given us a spirit of fear, but of power and of love and of a sound mind", "I can do all things through Christ who strengthens me", "It is the LORD who goes before you. He will be with you; he will not leave you or forsake you. Do not fear or be dismayed".

I imagined when the ghost would have gone, my bestie will return with her same mischievous charm, but instead I go into another dark valley of my dream, away from Querie and closer to Erik.

19.

My eyes feel heavy and watery. I rub my eyes with my human hands, fortunately! This time I didn't forget that I haven't left the game of dreams.

I let my eyes to look at my new hitch. I widen my eyes and revive the burden of my body to my legs as I observe where I am. My heart gives its way to my mind when my goose bumps surround my skin. It's another dream come true for me, yet in a dream.

I am standing in Sherlock Holmes' house.

I have been reading Sherlock Holmes since I first heard about his fictional character and Sir Arthur Conan Doyle's works 9 years ago.

I admire both the creator and the character for the different perceptions and the ways how they deal with the world and their hearts.

I used to watch the seasons of Sherlock Holmes so much, that I made an image of his house and that is what I can see in front of me. I can feel an air of mystery around me. One would suspect everything in Holmes' place.

My doubt ends after half an hour of rummaging his house. *I am really in Sherlock Holmes' house.* It has a refrigerator filled with blood and flesh. A violin kept near the window, accompanying a stand holding his self-composed notes. The center of the room has two arm-chairs, one for him and the other for his comrade, Dr. Watson. This couple can solve every mystery and unveil every suspense. Together, they can fasten your heartbeats and make your eyes stick on them and feel their suspense.

I suddenly realize that my observation power has grown. I can, now, observe every detail in depth of their presence. I can, now, find a story to my surroundings. I can, now, trace the right circumstances for right matter. I feel invincible.

A curtain that is not parted with the window for a long time, has made home for dust on it. A pair of moccasins, whose flipped positions can tell that they have been deserted in a hurry and have not been rescued from there since the curtains were opened. A coffee stain on the floor, whose color and smell tells me that it has been spilled while its drinker was captured from the very same place. Sherlock's black clay pipe lying on the wooden circular table between the two chairs. His pipe's smoke is recent than the dust on the shoes and the curtains.

I swirl at my place to look for any sign of my favorite fictional character. I find none.

I find stairs leading to the floor below. I take them and crash to the same old-looking black floating oval balloon, but this time, with a different price of escape from the previous level.

It read, 'Save Doctor Watson's life'.

"I suppose I am Sherlock Holmes as I have always imagined to be", I assume my awakening in my dream, and dance with happiness in the clothes and hat of Sherlock Holmes.

When I was in India, Nipun and I used to act detectives and solve fantasy mysteries and used all kinds of tools to stay original. But, this is not a play, my love's life is at stake here, and I need to indulge my Sherlock skills and senses to find my partner. I am the only person who can help myself.

A thrashing sound separates me from my memories and I run towards the door to watch the invasion of aliens.

Wait, what? Aliens? From where did the aliens come in Sherlock's world? Well, I am just kidding!

It's a wakeup call for me to go and find Dr. Watson. So, I follow the commotion outside 221B Baker Street. From one street to another, from one square to another, I have the capability to observe every brick of every house, every person hiding from my line of sight, every mark on the non-livings and every furrow of the wanderers. I could sense my surroundings through the best of my conscience.

I am led to a building about 8 floors high, mahogany colored, consisting of just a door on the ground floor and a window in my front on the topmost floor.

My sixth sense predicts that Dr. Watson has been kept as a hostage on the topmost floor. So I follow my instincts and walk through the silence of the wind on the pathway constructed between the grasses empowering my footsteps. I open the white-colored door and enter the mysterious inside world.

20.

When I was a young girl, I prayed about my future husband to be caring and loving and supportive, and I thought I found him in my early teens. There was a guy named Ralph Givhan. I found him at a party boozing and flirting. Since every girl had a crush on him, I too started finding him attractive. He had those dimples on his cheeks when he used to laugh. He used to show-off his fake medals and awards on his fake boxing competitions. He used to bite girls on their necks and lead them towards his room, and all I could hear from outside were the screams of those girls, and those screams were definitely a call for help, instead of being the screams of pleasure, he used to abuse their body.

It was yet another booze party and I was observing Ralph as he was flirting with me. I fell for his talks and thought that he was the love of my life. He was touching my hair and sliding his hands down towards my butt, while his other hand was rubbing my thighs. I was following him to his room, without my mind interrupting my moves, I was just kissing him and suffering his painful bites.

"Wait up, dude!", a voice halted me and that asshole from corrupting me. Still, my eyes were fixed on Ralph, waiting for him to make me his valuable asset. Yes, I was that crazy!

"That chick is asking for you", the voice continued. Ralph glanced back and forth towards me and whoever the voice was pointing to. Then, he squeezed my thighs, bit my neck and whispered, "Wait in my room, I will be back in a minute". I trusted him with my subconscious desperate needs and went into his room, waiting for him, half-naked, and ready to get in bed with him, completely naked.

After 5 minutes, I heard a knock on the door and turned my attention towards the intruder. I saw that voice having green eyes. He handed me a glass of water and said that Ralph wanted me to drink that. Since, I was in love with that jerk Ralph, I drank it and fainted on the bed.

The last thing I remembered were those beguiling green eyes.

21.

I enter the white door in my subconscious mind. My head decides to be the leader and my lower body, the follower, to confront with Ralph's house. I look around the hall for a couple of minutes to scrutinize my dream. There is no furniture, no curtains – well, there are no windows – no sign of any living Homo sapiens. There are stairs on my right, leading me towards my mission.

According to my Sherlock Holmes' instincts, this building is a trap, a labyrinth. It's a mind game.

I analyze every corner of the floor, every hidden hole in the wooden walls, every scratch and mark of the past, and all I find is that, this building has not sheltered any human since it has been built.

I decide to take the stairs to try and reach Watson. I reach the first floor. It is an identical twin of the ground floor. The interesting thing is that, when I turn around, I find the same white door which welcomed me into this maze.

I walk another step forward, and I find that the sound of my footsteps has the exact same frequency and pitch. *I am still on the ground floor. How can this be possible?*

To be able to answer myself, I decide to go upstairs again, from the stairs on my right, and I end up standing on another identical twin of the ground floor, with the white door behind me and same sound of my footsteps, depicting that I am still standing on the ground level.

There has to be a way out of this maze.

I use my knuckle, and knock the wooden walls every feet apart. The sound on every knock is the same, except one, below the stairs. It sounds as if there is another beginning to that barricade.

I use my elbow and break that wooden barrier, and crawl from under the darkness to the room.

"Not again!", I sigh as I reach yet another identical twin of that room.

I already figured out that this is a trap, and only mastering this trap can lead me to Erik, after leading me to Dr. Watson.

I sit with my eyes closed, my legs crossed, and revive to my Erik's time. His protective warmth, his shining eyes, his wet lips, his addictive touch, his optimism, his love. I have been alone all this time, but still he has been the one giving me the strength to move forward, reach him and escape together.

My hands wipe the tears from my eyes and map my way from entering the third level, to being Sherlock Holmes, to entering the building, to searching for Dr. Watson, to analyzing the wooden walls and floor of this labyrinth, and to reliving my past with Erik.

I can't find a way out. My tangled thoughts are planning a conspiracy against my weeping heart.

I retrace my observations of Ralph's house. The different sounds of wood, the neat flooring, and the ceiling... *The ceiling?*

I open my eyes with a spark and whisper to myself, "I didn't check the ceiling".

I stand up, my head perpendicular to my torso, and I am moving away from the white door to the stairs. There is a slight notch on the ceiling above the first stair, so I try and pull the rectangular plank. It clanks on the floor. I stretch my hand and search above the ceiling for any treasure. I feel a hard thin piece of wood. When I grab it, it feels heavier than a piece of wood and when I bring it near my torso, I see that it's a hammer, colored in brown.

"Now what?", I put the hammer in front of me to get an idea of my future actions. After a moment, I get a million dollar idea, "I can kill that cranky old man with this and skip my levels to meet Erik", my elation drowns with the same speed as it soared. I revert my concentration on Ralph's maze.

I walk on every wooden plank below my foot, lingering on the sounds of my steps. There is no difference between them; I do it again, the result being the same. I return to my meditation point, and there it is.

I tap my foot on that point and I can hear it. There is a sound of hollowness beneath it. A sound of the unknown. A sound for my enlightening hope.

I stab that plank, with the brown-colored hammer, again and again, letting out all my frustration and anger, murdering that piece of plank, until the smell of sea calls for me on another adventure.

There's water!

I love swimming, and I can sense it ahead of me. I remove Sherlock Holmes' attire until I am wearing just a black bra and an underwear, I take a long breathe, hold it and jump into my escape.

I am under-water, and I am loving it.

I am swimming and summersaulting and living the silence. The silence of everything accept my deep self. I have been craving for this silence since he left me on the prom night.

I swim for around an hour, moving forward with the stream of water, under the tube-shaped container, when I see a source of light in the darkness of my life, giving me the hope for a hand to hold on to.

I swim to the end of the tube, imagining Erik to be standing there, waiting for me, to get out of the water and combine my soul with his, but as I knew, there is no one else but my wet revealing body.

I see a white door ajar, calling me and so I walk towards it.

Across the door, there is a hall of mirror. I can see infinite me, wet, half naked. My blonde hair responding to the gravitational force, the water dripping over the black glassy floor, and my brown eyes, as hopeful as they were in the beginning of the game of dreams.

I can see myself all around myself. My white skin, blonde hair, long legs, bare feet, looking through my own eyes, finding for a way out, stuck in my own dreams.

At this moment, I have an epiphany; I am not Sherlock Holmes, I am as much myself as I can be. I was in his attire, but still, I was all *me*. I can feel my brain merging with my heart to understand my true self.

The hall of mirrors reflects the true me. I am trapped, yet I am emancipated, trapped in the hall of mirror, and emancipated from the matrix of my mind.

It was Erik who saved me, it was his green eyes that I remembered all this time. How could I not see this before! I have stared at his eyes a billion times, and I missed this! He was the one who saved me from losing my integrity with Ralph. He has always been the one whose eyes I have admired. He have always been *The One* for me.

"I love you even more, Erik, and now I need you even more", these levels are destroying me slowly, playing with my mind and heart at the same time. I can't think pragmatically in my dreams.

I need to conquer my mental peace to escape to Erik, I need to fight this war alone, for Erik!

I gather myself, intake the watery air and move towards my reflection in the center of the mirror hall, forming brume on the glass between my two mouths, and listen to the disturbance of the silence, the sound of my breathe.

I become a detective again and knock at every mirror between my infinite reflections, and find the same hollow response from every one of them.

I analyze the hall from its feet to its abyss head, and I find nothing suspicious.

This level is a complete trap. First, it trapped my mind over Sherlock Holmes, then the labyrinth of Ralph's home, and then this entrapment of mirrors.

When I analyzed the roof, I saw a black hole, there was only darkness and loneliness, and no escape or hope for love.

My task is to find Dr. Watson. Since I am not Sherlock Holmes, then where will I find Watson? He has always been Sherlock's comrade, and I can see neither of them here.

I am frozen in between my shivering reflections, in the center of the mirror hall, lost in myself, desperate to reach Erik. *I hope Erik's fine!* I don't know what Gablet is, what it wants from us, or why both of us are ensnared in it, all I know is I have to find Erik and save us both.

I need to think clearly.

I sit on my black glassy reflection coming from the floor, my legs crossed, my eyes closed and I revert to my entrails.

Here goes nothing!

"The first level… nothing. The second level… nothing. The third level… being Sherlock… Ralph's labyrinth… water tube… mirror hall… the present…", I soliloquize.

Nothing.

"I don't understand it. I need you Erik", I whisper, looking at my reflection.

Find Dr. Watson.

I close my eyes again, and find the true answer, "There is no Sherlock Holmes. It was me from the beginning. What if Dr. Watson has also been an illusion from the start? What if Watson is also me?"

22.

I am pulled into a deep black dream. My subconscious mind tells me that I should not move a muscle. I am exhausted, so, I stretch and sleep on a soft bed, my savior from my stress.

My tiredness wears out and I open my eyes after anonymous hours. The morning light welcomes me in my own room, my colorful room, and not my green room.

Sleep makes your subconscious mind stronger, so much stronger that I was going to follow my real-world schedule, till I didn't find my Indian slippers. Suddenly, I feel Erik's sensation and realize that I need to save him and I am still in the game of dreams.

I let my pupils stress on my surroundings, and there is no sign of his body, or his belongings.

I shouldn't fool myself like this! I can't leave this game so easily, the price to be paid is much higher.

I stretch my arms, breathe in the fragrance of fresh morning air and start towards the lavatory.

I halt before the door, only to catch another girl bathing in it, water showering her bare body, like the blessings from the God. Her golden hair changed its color to dark gold and her skin reflecting the sparkles from the water. Her hands moving from her face to her head. Her hips perfectly curved from her thighs to belly, white as an angel.

I turn around, embarrassed from her nakedness and shout, overpowering the shower's noise, "Who are you, and what are you doing in my bathroom?"

I wait for a minute, with a hope, but get no response.

"Answer me, or I will expose you!", I shout again.

I wait, this time, for more than a minute, and still get no response as an award.

I clench my teeth, move out to the bed, and sit there, waiting for her to cover her nakedness and answer me.

I look at the ceiling, and there is no pseudo-sky wallpaper. I look at my left, and there is no laptop on the table. I look at my right, and there isn't any of my photo frames, but there's a photo of a girl who looks just like me. Her hair, the same blonde layers; her eyes, the same cunning brown; her skin color, the same adorable white; but not the same nose, chin, jawline...

The girl is standing in front of me, with black jeans and blue full-sleeves top, with 'Love the way you are' printed on it in black, accompanying silhouettes of three jumping girls.

Why does she look similar?

She is busy packing her bag, ignoring my existence.

"Don't you ignore me! Who are you? Where am I? Answer me", I am standing just behind her, while she is busy avoiding me and arranging her books in her bag.

I lift my right arm to cup her shoulder with my palms, and my eyes widen and my jaws drop. My arm went past her opaque body right in front of my eyes.

I try to touch her, at least 10 more times, and she goes on doing her business, stalked by an invisible girl.

"Am I dead?", my heart skips a beat, my throat dries, and my head feels heavy. *If I am dead, then I have failed to escape Erik from his dreams, and now what? Will I become insane? What will happen to Erik?*

I am standing in that girl's way to downstairs, she walks towards me and then through me. *She just walked through me.* I am a ghost in her world.

"Who is she?", my furrowed eyebrows narrow down to her frame.

"She is your mother", it's the cranky old man. I shift my gaze from the photo frame to the study table, and there he is, standing near the table, in a *lungi*. I have seen Indians wear this a few times.

"What, in the world, are you wearing?", he is a complete attention-seeker.

"Really? You are concerned about my attire at present?", he tilt his black head and gives a fool's expression.

"Yeah… Okay… Never mind!", I wave my hand, erasing my last question, and continue with my bedlam state, "Who was that girl?"

"As I already answered… She is your mother", as he replies, my imagination makes its way to the answers and echoes in my ears, *that's why she looked so familiar!*

"But how can she be my mother? She is of my age!", I say this more to myself than to the cranky old man.

"Just go peek into her life", he says and vanishes in the air of dreams.

"Finish your breakfast, young lady!", a lady's voice travelled from downstairs to my ears.

I follow the voice to the stairs. My mother's photo frame is hanging in between the way. She is in a red sleeveless top, black draped skirt, red stilettos, red lipstick, with a black hobo bag, showing off her beauty at… a church? It seems like a white church; she is smirking at somebody, besides the camera-person, her eyes are amused at the sight, but her face maintains her grace; her hair still and perfectly curved at the ends.

I move a couple of stairs forward and look at another wall photo frame with a family of three. My mother in between, aged about 13 years, and her parents on either sides, with one arm on her either shoulders. The family in black! My grandmother seems more beautiful than my mother; her golden hair longer and silkier than my mother or mine, touching her waist, and her smile mesmerizing her husband. My grandfather seems an adorable and loving father, his eyes reserved for his family and his own world. I predict that he would have been a one-of-a-kind artist of his era.

"I am leaving", I run down as I realize my mother exiting from her home. This home is twain to my house; the differences are minute, including photos, electronics and lifestyle.

I glance at my grandmother, she, still, is a beauty but with a shorter hair.

I never had the fortune of being pampered by any of my grandparents. My father became an orphan when he was 2, and my mother became one when I was a month old.

23.

Her hair is wavering, her hips matching her steps, showing off their untouched value. I know, I shouldn't describe my mother like this, but she is definitely sexier than I have ever been. She may be 16 at present.

Wherever we walk, all guys shift their gaze to her. She is not exposing anything, this defines a woman's true beauty.

She is carrying a bunch of books between her arms and her breasts, a yellow shoulder bag matching her lemon top. Her face is glowing from her narcissism, moving rhythmically with the tune in her head.

A bunch of people are playing basketball on our left side behind the fence, and we walk past them when one of them notices my mother and comments, "Oh Katrina! Your beauty needs to be corrupted by my dirty moves. Come to me, Katrina!"

She moves out of her mental world, into the disgusting reality. She avoids that brawn commenter and keeps moving to her destination.

I can see lust in the red-headed commenter. Other players join his commentary and starts making kissing noises howling like a pack of dogs, but worse than dogs.

I pick up my pace as my mother does. I can feel the fear arousing within her little beautiful world.

"Go run, girl! But tonight will be our night!", a long-haired brawn with French accent shouted, and they start laughing like basketball-playing demons.

We pass that court almost running, as if going far away from the reality, and almost all the way after that till we reach my mother's school. I don't recognize the state. I am sure that we are in USA, by observing the lifestyle of the people, but can't figure out the exact place. I can't even find an address plate that can tell my exact location, so I stick with my mother until she attends all her classes in her school.

I don't follow her in her classes, rather I lay on the grass in the playground of her school. The blue sky embraces my soul, the birds fly to their loved ones and slowly, I get lost in my past.

24.

The lonesome ride ended when I stopped playing around and looked at my watch. I couldn't see anything but my own shadow. Couldn't see myself in me. I have lost something of mine, something precious, but I can't seem to remember what it is.

I look around myself and there is nobody to answer me. I am running to someone, to something, that could tell me my way.

That wasn't me, that was someone else. I wanted to find myself. I wanted to be myself again.

I halted at the bus station and found a dog trying to survive through the food from the garbage.

I took out my sandwich from my bag, unwrapped the foil and gave it to him. He was more than grateful and I could see only love in his eyes.

I was getting late. Time was running faster than usual.

I let go of my *amore* and moved towards the bus. I didn't seem to remember where it would take me, all I remember is that I needed to move faster, I needed to run faster than I was at that time.

I glanced at the eating dog and sat on an empty seat beside a pregnant lady.

Why was I running? Is it okay to be a coward sometimes?

The bus revved and my heartbeat started beating faster, with my bumbled up mind. I was confused. Was I taking the right step?

The bus was made silent by   some outsiders. They called me by my name, and I was rescued at the right time.

I was 6 years old at that time and I ran away to find my real father. I eavesdropped my mother and my stepfather talking about my real father and that they were providing legal protection to me.

Safety from my own father? I thought at that time, why would a child need protection from her own father? Why hasn't he come looking for me? Doesn't he love me? Or has my stepfather done something bad to him?

I was forced back to stay at my home, grounded, or was that even my home at that time?

I was told, 'your father is a very bad person and did bad things to your mother'. They didn't describe what he did, or how bad he was.

All I was made to agree was that I would never try to find my real father again, otherwise, my mother would cry and become very sad.

Over time, I accepted my stepfather to be my father as he loved me more than anyone in the whole world; he is definitely more than my real father, and I stopped asking my mother or father about the bad things of my biological father.

I can relive the day when I caught pneumonia. I thought I would die. I had heard so many news of children dying of it, so I asked my father, "Daddy?"

"Yes, angel?"

"Am I going to die?", I was lying on the hospital bed then.

He cupped my palm with his, smiled and said, "I won't let you part me. Even if God comes and asks me if he can spend time with you, I would order him to stay away from you, tell him that you are my angel, and he can find someone else to spend time with. But I will never let him part you from me. Alright sweety?"

I saw my father's smile and tears together for the first time.

The next day, I opened my eyes to see both my parents sitting beside me and talking about my biological father. They were discussing my mother's fate while she was crying and mumbling the truth behind my birth. I tried hard to listen to every word, but my subconscious mind contained it instead and I went back into a deep sleep.

25.

I wish I could get back the time that I wasted in hating my stepfather and finding my biological father, and replace them with the love for him. But time is a bitch! You can't bring it back, and neither can you play with it. You have to wait for the right time, it won't fly to you, but it can disappear in the nights' shadow.

I fall asleep, and I am awakened by music, guitar strumming somewhere behind me. I turn around to find the origin of the melody, and I find a crowd encircling the player.

I stand up and start towards the music, and the player is a beautiful singer as well. I join the crowd and see my mother sitting beside the melodious soul.

Her eyes are changing their direction from her beautiful young neighbor to the crowd and to his black acoustic dreadnought Gibson. The words to the talking strings are,

Don't let me go away,

To the world far away,

I am meant to be,

With you…

Oh…oh…

Like a song to the beats.

You wanna fly with me?

In the space of love,

Where you and I,

Will fall again…

In love.

Be the beat to my song,

Let our heartbeats beat in unison,

(Heartbeats beat… o… heartbeats…)

Look there's a falling star,

Mimicking our love,

Coming to the Earth,

Bringing love…

To the hearts…

Which beats…

Like you and me…

Like a song to the beats…

Then he hums, and strums. My mother stands up, kisses the guy on his cheek, picks up her books, makes way through the humming crowd, and starts walking down the street.

I follow her through the pathway to a café named 'Beans'. She reaches the cashier, greets her, exchanges remarks and switches to her post.

The new cashier is the blonde girl, my beautiful and smart mother, in a black apron.

I sit at the corner-most table and observe her till 7 in the evening. Her calculations are fast, unlike mine. She doesn't even need the calculator. She is always shining and smiling to her customers, unlike the way she is in the real present world. Something has changed her, made her aloof. She is the most beaming cashier I have ever seen. She remembers the patrons and their orders. She treats every person as that person is the most special.

Man! I want to be like her!

A black guy comes at sharp 7, embraces her and switches to her post.

"Sorry for being late", the black guy apologizes as my mother hurries to pick up her stuff.

"Tomorrow, sharp 6.30!", she flies out the café and her tail, that is me, with her.

It's dark outside and my mother soliloquy, worrying that she will reach home late, again! We reach the same eerie basketball court, but this time,

there was no one to insult her purity, just the silence
of the unsafe street.

26.

"Please don't! I beg you. Leave me. Please, leave me", the cries of a young girl echo the basketball court.

"AAAAHHHH... Someone help me", the wails are unheard to any decent human being.

They stuff a cloth in her mouth and all she can do is make covert cries.

There are three brawn basketball players. They have tethered her hands and legs, and are tearing apart her clothes. She is trying to crawl away, but the one with the black hair has a good hold of her.

The leaner one opens the zip of his pants, pull down his pants and underwear, tear apart my mother's and lays on her.

He tears up her brassiere, sucks her breasts, and starts pushing himself in her, inserting his penis the hardest possible way into her untouched and pure body, destroying her soul.

I can see her helpless tears crawling through her cheeks, her fitful moans seeking for an escape. Her blood is flowing to see the tough reality, and the player is laughing, grinning, and sucking.

I am shouting, knocking through the doors, trying to hit the rapists, but I am invisible, I don't exist here, and I can't help her, I can just sit there and watch her sufferings, listen to her moans. I look to the dark sky,

"Please save her. Don't do this to her. Don't do this to me", and there is no star or moon to give a ray of hope to me.

"Move, it's my turn now", the one with the orange t-shirt yells, waiting to have his part of fun.

"I have just started, wait for 5 more, then she will be all yours", he is busy moving his part inside and outside, making my mother stir her whole body.

I listen the distant sirens of cops. I run towards it, and it's headed to my mother. Fortunately, someone has called them for help.

The basketball players panic, leave my mother unconscious, numb, lying alone on the red ground.

I wipe my tears and keep my ears to her naked breast. Her heartbeats are weakening.

"Please come fast, she is about to die. Hurry, please, hurry!", I yell to the cops, but they can't hear me. I know the whole story, but I can't tell them, I can't bring justice to my mother.

I go back, when she was racing with time to her home. She didn't notice three guys stalking her. I was trying to warn her, but she couldn't listen to an invisible soul.

The guy who yelled for his chance before, got his hands to her mouth and dragged her to the eerie basketball court. The other two held my mother firmly, pulling her hair, bringing more pain to her kidnapping, and with time, that kidnapping became raping.

I was there the whole time. I tried everything, kicking on the nuts of those assholes, shouting at the center of the streets, reaching the penetrating doors near the basketball court, but I couldn't do anything to save her from that excruciating agony.

This will break her into pieces, in the number of pieces that will be impossible to count.

27.

I am holding her hands, virtually. She is being operated in the OT, and the blood from her lower body is hard to stop. I close my eyes and sing her the same lullaby that she used to sing to me when I was a kid.

"This shouldn't have happened! Why did this happen to her? She is so young. How cruel can one be!", I murmur to myself.

"Let's fly with time", the cranky old man's voice is followed by twirls, darkness and similar scenario.

My hands are cupped to my mother's palm, penetrating her opaque body. She is sleeping in a hospital, and she seems to glow, but looks exhausted.

A baby's cry wakes her up. The nurse puts the baby in her arms, my mother smiles at the baby, kisses her on her forehead and says, "How's my little Rachel?"

It's me! My mother is weeping the tears of joy. Her face is glowing, while her eyes are crying. Her eyes are joyous, while her lips tremble. This moment is ineffable. A moment that is the beacon of a new beginning and a new end.

I was never told the story of my birth, except for the name of the hospital. Now I understand why they kept it a mystery! I was an unwanted and heartbreaking fusion of ovary and sperm. I am the result of a rape.

I cry. Not because I am a result of disgust, but because my mother accepted me even though she was physically and emotionally torn.

I have always loved my mother, but now, I look at her with admiration and affection of being stronger than any person I have ever met or heard of.

She prepares to feed me, while I see all her bruises are still fresh and clear. The bruises on her neck, stomach, breasts; they all are evidence of my existence in this world.

The sucking sound continues and I give them the mother-daughter time and head to the door, penetrating through it. I don't see my grandmother or my grandfather.

Why haven't they come yet?

I return to the room and both were asleep. My mother and little me.

"She is very weak. This was not the right time for her to give birth to another soul", the doctor is talking to a lady.

"But she has made a miracle!", the lady interrupts.

"Yes, she has! But you need to take intense care of her", the doctor orders.

"Yes doctor, I will", the lady replies.

"Is there anyone else with her? Her family?", the doctor asks, turning the pages of my mother's reports.

"No. Just me!", the lady prompts.

The lady gains the doctor's attention. He looks at her with question marks flying between them.

The lady continues, "She did it against her parent's will".

The doctor nods and passes from my left side to the exit.

I am all that she gets.

The lady goes near the little me. She sets back my mother's black hair from the front of her eyes to the back of her ear, and looks at me, worried.

She didn't choose to kill me.

I smile and kiss my mother on her forehead, and everything vanishes, just like a dream.

28.

My head aches. My throat is soar. I am lying on something hard. I am lying as if hugging myself. My human hands and legs are in front of me, and they are green.

I stand, using my green arm as a stick and look around myself. I have visited this place before, in my dream.

I am living my green dream!

The street is where I live, but it's green. Everything's green. If someone would tell me to describe my green dream, I would say that imagine your eyesight is passing through a color filter, making you color blind, with an exception that you can see only green color.

I look around, with goose bumps. I am in my nightmare, soon I will be confronting my biggest fear.

I walk down the green road to his green house. *This is level 5. He would be waiting for me in his room.*

I sense butterflies in my stomach. I run to the porch and open the front door, enter the green house, skip two stairs at a time, reach his room and smash it open.

"Erik!", I pant and smile, and I stampede. It was not Erik. There was just one other green person in the whole house. It is me. The sleeping me.

I look at myself, lying on Erik's bed, eyes closed, hugging his photo frame.

"This can't be happening", my forehead secretes water and I feel like standing between burning flames.

I wiggle backwards and run out of the house. I keep running on the road till I reach my green house. It's empty. I feel hollow from inside.

I look to the green sky and shout the words, standing on my green porch, "Where are you, Erik?"

I ask for the cranky old man, ask for the flying balloon, shout to have the answers, and all I get is a green silence.

I sigh, "There is no harmony. Just mess".

I need to relax. I sit down on the green stairs, close my eyes and concentrate on my breathing. Inhale. Exhale.

"Pssssst", I turn around to the voice.

"Pssst", it's coming from the basement.

I stand up and walk towards the voice. My green house's basement is calling to me. I follow the 'psst' and bend in front of the green glass of the basement.

I see a green creature with green eyes. It's a human. It's Erik.

I run into the house, to the basement and jump on green Erik, hugging and kissing him.

I am hanging on him, my legs wrapping his waist, my hands on his hair and my lips tasting him.

"Never ever do that again", I cry and hug him as tight as I can.

"Never", he whispers.

He carries me to the green couch, with me still hanging like an ape, and we sit hugging each other for quite a time.

He pulls my face in his palms, and there are tears in my eyes, I am sobbing.

"I am sorry, Raech. Please don't cry", his eyes start to show tears.

I kiss him, he lays backwards, with me on his top. He shifts his hands from my face to my stomach, slowly and seductively. He moves his cold hands on my green back, removes my green top and unstraps my green bra. I remove his green shirt, and we make ourselves completely naked. Our green skin exchange all the love we have in us.

The color of harmony proves itself to be the right color of love.

We sleep for anonymous glorious hours on the floor. We slipped down to the floor from the couch in between, and we didn't even notice.

Thump… thump…

The tremors hit Erik's sleep and he wakes me up.

"What is that?", I ask, covering my green body with my green top.

"Probably a dinosaur", he answers, pulling his green jeans to his waist and going towards the basement window.

I put my clothes on and join his fear.

"Do you know my greatest fear?", I ask him, looking for any sign for my greatest fear.

"Dinosaur?", he turns towards me, with his shining green eyes, as if he has found answers to all his questions.

I nod, but with a furrowed brow, well, he got me all confused.

"Now I understand why they are here", he continues, looking straight in my eyes.

"What do you mean?", I ask. I have unending questions, but one at a time would do.

"The dinosaurs were not here before today. We are living our greatest fears in the last level. The fear that has been lying within us the deepest, and we have been hiding them under our soul for years. The game wants us to confront our deepest and greatest fears. So, either we would lose or we would conquer our fears", his hands move from his head, waves in the air, trying to make me understand and imagine my green dream, "This is the last level, and the deepest level of our subconscious mind. It will show the thing that can most affect our heart and destroy us from the core".

I look at him, blankly. *Is he saying what I think he is saying?*

"What is your greatest fear?", I ask him with all the energy left in me after the green dream's web.

"Green", he replies.

I stare back at him with questions hanging between him and me.

"I am afraid of the green color", he elaborates.

I stare at him, eyebrows raised, eyes wide and mouth open.

"Don't look at me like that. It's called chlorophobia, the fear of color green, and… it's a long story why I became afraid of it", he tries not to make a fool of himself.

"Yeah… let's hear it out", I sit on the couch, with my hands supporting my chin.

"Fine", he sighs and sits next to me.

"My grandmother was a great person. She loved me the most and I loved her the most. She used to call me her bobtail", he gives a smile, reliving his past on his left green wall, "as I used to follow her everywhere," his smile fades as fast as it appeared, "It was May 9. I was visiting her on the weekend. I was going to give her birthday present. Yes! It was her

107

birthday", there are tears filling his eyes, "I knocked on her door, and found it ajar, so I let myself in to surprise her. I walked in her room, and the green paint was lying all over the room, covering her dead body on the ground. I shouted for help, called an ambulance, but her soul had already left her body. She had had a heart attack, and I don't know for how much time she had squirmed…", he started wailing.

"Only if I would have visited her earlier, she would have… been alive", he continues, sobbing and crying and whispering.

I take him in my arms and try to soothe him. My eyes are filling with tears.

After a couple of minutes, he says, "Do you know what I brought her as her birthday present?"

I shake my head.

"Two tickets for Miami", he pauses and continues, "She always used to complain for wasting her life by not having visited there. So I decided to spend my summers with her in Miami. But, she left me", he ceases.

"That's why I am afraid of color green. It pulls me to my past. Breaks me every time I bring myself together", he takes control of himself and pulls himself apart from my embrace and stands up.

"I am sorry", I whisper.

"Don't be. Now let's think about conquering our fears and get the hell out of this bullshit game", he tries to pull himself out of his tragedy, uncasing his anger towards the torcher of this game of dreams.

He takes my hand, pulls me up from the couch and kisses me on my lips.

"I love you", he says, "Even the green you".

"Me too", I blush and kiss him again on his lips, "And I promise to make you chlorophobia resistance".

29.

"Say something", I say.

He gathers all his courage and replies, "I can't".
"Erik?"

He looks me in my eyes.

"Do you trust me?", I ask.

"More than myself", he prompts.

"Then we are going to win our greatest fears together", I hold his hand, moving my thumb across his knuckles.

He smiles, nods and then sighs, "But how?"

I tell him about my green dream and how I burned that green beast and the world became colorful again, and then, how I died.

The last part was funny for me, but I know the drill, if I die this time, I am not going to survive the real world sanely.

"I won't let anything happen to you", Erik says, as if reading my mind.

I smile.

"Let's burn that dinosaur?", he asks, offering his hand to me, proposing to get into the real world.

I accept his offer and we head out to the green streets.

"You know, I feel so much better with you. I was losing myself, surrounded by my green past. You gave me strength, and a reason to carry on", he says as we walk on the street, searching for the dinosaur.

"I am glad I helped", I smiled, masking my fear. *I am going to meet a dinosaur, how am I going to face him?*

"Raech?", Erik calls.

"Yes"

"I am here with you. We are going to be alright", he stops me and hugs me. We both are living our scariest fears, he knows how it feels.

I hug him back, but with full of adrenaline rush, "We should practice the green spit".

He parts me away and say, "Okay… then… let's burn… that house", he points to my left.

It was someone's elegant green house.

"Not that one", I say, "That's so beautiful".

"Babe? We are in a dream", he is right.

"I know… But let's burn that one?", I point to my North-east. I never liked that house. It seems evil and depressing and as if made by serial-killers. I never liked its ambience.

Erik has no choice but to agree with me. We walk towards the house and stand a feet away from that evil green going-to-be-history house.

We collect all the saliva in our mouth and spit with all the force left in our green bodies.

The green sphere touches the house's porch and burns it, with green flames spreading into fire. The flames are dancing on the tune of destruction, and the fire is hugging through the walls, welcoming itself to the inside world of that dislikable house.

We run away from the hot waves emitted by the screaming greenery, saving our lives. Erik suddenly stops and turns his head to look at the reaction of our action, when I see tears in his eyes.

He was reliving his past, but this time it was vivid, coming to life in the form of tale-telling flames.

I hold his hand and say, "We need to move on!"

He peeks at the fire and we run away to our new faithful escape.

30.

"How did I cross the first level?", I ask Erik as we walk on the green streets, searching for the monstrous green beast.

"What do you mean?", he asks.

"In my first level, the task given to me was to kill Lindsey, but I didn't even touch her, instead I saved her soul", I explain, recalling my combat with the colorful tiger.

"Really?", he asks, predicting his own theories.

I went in the memories of my first level, and Erik lost in his own thoughts.

My task was to kill Lyndsey, but Lindsey is my bitch, and she turned into a human in the game. And, I was some kind of a dog. Why was I a dog? Or is it..?? Is this the reason? I was Lindsey? But that girl whispered that the name Lindsey in my ears, or was she telling me who I was?

"I was Lindsey", I yell.

"What?", he revives into the present.

"In my first level, I was Lindsey. When I saved that girl, the tiger killed me. That means, I killed Lindsey", I mumble out.

"What girl? What tiger?", he asks.

"Oh, it's a long story. I will tell you all about it, but first we need to get out of here", I smirk, but I know he also has his part of story to tell me.

We head forward to find a dinosaur to burn, and in my mind, I think of ways to make Erik get out of his past, to make him conquer the green color, then only we could see the colorful world again.

"The night before the prom night, I wore a green top, and you were held back for a moment. I remember that expression of yours clearly. I assumed that you expected someone else. You were struck on my appearance. I asked you about it, and you just jumped on me, hugged me sobbing. But after a while, you were not bothered by it. I was throwing my top on you, and you didn't even flinch. How did you conquer your fear that night?", I ask as if I have a flight to catch.

His eyes flutter away from me, recalling the night and his reaction to his fear.

"I was so much into you, I forgot everything, my past, my grief, and all I knew was that I had the most beautiful and amazing girl in my arms, well, apart from this that she was mocking my romantic gestures", he smiles and I laugh so loud, that a nearby dinosaur can kill me of my weird laugh.

"I love you", his gaze goes right through my cornea and makes me want to cry.

I hug and kiss him, slamming our bodies on the green road.

"Close your eyes", I whisper in his ears.

He closes them without another word. He trusts me more than I can trust myself. I smile and kiss him intermittently, whispering to him, "You need to love me so much... that when you see the color green... instead you see me".

He opens his eyes, peeking through my green hair, binding them with his hands, and whispers along with the rhythm of my racing heartbeats,

"We are together

No one can part us

You love me

Like I love you

You are my soul

And I your heartbeats

You are my reason

You are my fate

I will love you

Love you like you have never been loved

I will love you

Love you with all the passion in me"

I kiss him, caress his hair, and whisper, "Never again leave me like that. Never again break my heart", and start crying in his arms.

"You were holding this back since we met, I wanted you to take everything out. Stop being strong and feel how much I was incomplete without you. I, too, was broken into pieces", his eyes reflect green tears.

He holds me like never before. He knows how much I need him, he knows how I felt when he was gone. I was being strong ever since he left me. He knows it's time to end that pretense. I don't know how he came to know that, but he knows it was time for me to cry in his arms as long as I can.

I cry till all my tears dry out and he holds me till I force him to pull back, look at me and kiss me.

"I think we should kill our fears instead of making out", he laughs.

I give way to laughter and he gives way to a smug. *Yeah, he is the one who made me cry and made me smile.*

I close my eyes and hug him until I knew that he will always be with me, no matter how I feel, no matter what the life brings to us, I know he will never betray me.

When I open my eyes, the color of harmony has already given up to make way to the beautiful colors of life. I feel beauty inside me, I feel the inner peace, not brought by the color of harmony, but brought by the light of love.

His green eyes are not scary, but naturally glowing by the colors of my brightness.

"You look better when you are not covered in green", he pulls me closer, grabbing my waist. His smell is magical. My lips touches his, my tongue touches his, and I get a taste that is far away from my fear.

31.

Life is much more than your fear or love. It is a combination of all that you can do and you think you can't do. It is a challenge to your limits. I found my life when someone grew over one's greatest fear because of love. It made me realize the importance of being loved, the power of light over dark, the reason to believe in fantasy, and make it your reality.

"Now, it's time for me to conquer *my* fear", I look ahead, my back straight, my eyes fixed on the green Stegosaurus, this time the green is dinosaur's natural color.

I go forward, lose the grip of Erik's hand, and enter into the reality of my dream. I am standing few feet from him, he is a tall beast with alienated eyes, and I revive to my death. I twirl my hair to look at Erik, he has crossed his fingers, his eyes are longing for my victorious return and his posture is ready to save me from the falling dinosaur.

I face towards my target, collect my saliva, and get ready to *kaboom* him, when I see that he is not even trying to attack me. He is standing in front of me like a petted dog, but with less enthusiasm and exhilaration. I bring my right hand forward, as if I am waiting my motherly love to touch the inner child of dinosaur. I don't know what I am doing, all I feel is, this dinosaur won't harm me, and I can't harm an innocent.

"Raech", Erik calls to me and I keep moving forward.

"Rachel don't", he yells and I am an inch away from my green pet.

Erik runs towards me as I bring love to my fear. I feel Erik's hand touch mine, and we return to the dark conveyance.

32.

My body is cupped in someone else's, I fly open my eyes to enter the real world with my love in my arms. I hug him more tightly and he hugs me till I am unable to breathe.

"Welcome back to our world", he says. I beg him not to kill me out of coziness, and like a merciful prince, he releases me from his strength.

"I need to go", I say as his questioning eyes demand an answer for my unexpected response.

"I won't do that again", his innocent response makes me chuckle. I kiss him on his lips, a quick but ardent kiss, run out of his room yelling that I need to go to India.

33.

India! The country of numerous religions. Here, if you pass a few miles in the same state, you will hear a different accent, and avail different lifestyle. India has its own cons, but still it is one of the most beautiful destinations to create golden memories.

In my tiresome journey to Shimla, I think all about Gablet. What is it? How did it trap Erik? How can one pill control the fate of your real world? I went through my first level to the last moment of Gablet. Starting from my heartbreak, and ending with a fairy tale story. Still I don't get an answer. *I need to discuss this with Erik, and go into the depth of the puppeteers of the game. They can't just mess up with people's minds like that.*

I catch an *auto-rickshaw* and move through the crowded mall road of Shimla to the beauty of nature, in between the ill-treated horses of Kufri, through the narrow wandering roads, into the clandestine bungalow-cum-farmhouse of Nipun.

My mother seems like a woman in black, in search for a soul to quench her thirst. Her hair is covering her face, her attire is black from top to bottom, and she is doing something with the mud.

"Mom", I call and run towards her and hug her as tightly as I hugged Erik, and she hugs me back, but with the embrace of gentle motherly love.

"What are you doing here?", she is surprised since I am not the kind of person who expresses her emotions easily, "Is everything fine? You fine?", she checks out my face, my clothes, my body, for any unfortunate sign of brutal world, and gladly she doesn't find any.

I start crying, hug her and sob until I let out my sentiments, "I am sorry for everything… I am sorry for the time I shouted at you… I am sorry that I complained when you asked for my company in your lonely time… I am sorry that I shouted at you unnecessarily… when you protected me from the basketball players… I am sorry when you cared for me… and I was being mean… I am sorry for everything mom… I am sorry!"

"It's okay baby. Everything's okay", she says, and suddenly her subconscious mind brings my words 'basketball players' into her conscious present and she clutches my shoulders, bringing me forward and asks me, "Did anyone hurt you? Did any basketball player do anything to you?"

"No mom, I am fine, everything's fine", I say as I wipe my tears from my face and transform my blurred vision to a limpid one. My mother was crying with me, and I decide to answer her enquiring eyes. My doubtful eyes glance at my dirty shoes, pull back the obstructing hair behind my ears, and relieve myself from the secret, "I…".

"Rachel…", my head turns back to look at my best friend and I hug him with the same intimation as I did with my mother.

I cry and laugh at the same time.

He pulls me to make me face him, "What's the matter? Is everything okay? Why are you crying?"

My mother puts her hand on my shoulder, making me turn towards her, and waiting for me to expose my heart to her. *She won't believe me.*

When my answer is silence and I stare unflagging on the muddy ground, my mother asks, "Who mentioned basketball players to you?"

"I just found out".

"Found out what?", she demands.

"Ab… About what happened to you! Why you always warned me to stay away from the basketball players! How I was born!", my voice depletes in every other sentence I say.

Her eyes opens wide in shock, "Who told you?"

I peek at confused Nipun and again to my demanding mother, "Does it matter? What matters is that now I love you even more".

She doesn't fall for my flattery, "Yes, it does matter. Now answer me, who told you?"

I try to use my mischievous mind and make up a story, "I… umm… found a paper in the basement telling all about that incidence".

She drifts away mentally, as if recalling her mistake, "You found it?"

"Yeah", I am completely blank on what paper she is talking about, but I am glad my fake story worked.

"I am sorry kiddo, it came to you like this", her eyes start showing the signs of her past sufferings into tears.

"It's alright mom, it's gone. We are all here with you", I soothe her. She tells me her soul-breaking journey, how my grandparents died, how I enlightened her world, and how my parents fell in love because of me.

"Where's dad?", my hair danced with my head trying to search for my father.

"Umm… Nipun's father and he have gone into the city for some work", she explains.

After satisfying my famished self, Nipun and I go through the back door, to his place of wandering, the log covered with the memories of him, Lindsey, the killer tiger, and my death.

Shimla is a beautiful city. Its nature can bring life to even the dead, no doubt my father has found peace in his awful work here.

"I tried reaching you. You didn't respond after your mother came here, and it has been 5 days. Is everything fine? Are you okay?",Nipun has been my best friend since my childhood, and I love the way he worries for me.

"I am more than okay", my huge smile makes him smile more than me, "Erik didn't ditch me. He was trapped… well… somewhere. We are back together", I continue.

My eyes are on the ground, the ground where I fought the tiger, where I was acquainted with the rules of a psychological game. *What is* *Gablet?*

"That's really great Raech", he says, without looking at me, I turn my eyes towards him, and all I see is fake happiness.

"What is it? Is everything alright?", I ask him.

"Everything's fine", he replies in his Indian accent, expressionless.

"Tell me Sonu, what is it?", my brows come together to avail my worry to Nipun.

"It's about your father", he is still looking at his brown floaters.

"What about my father?", I distract his sight by standing in front of him.

He takes my hands into his and with difficulty, answers, "He is in a sanatorium".

PART 2

1.

These past six months have been difficult for me, losing my grandmother, and being discernible about some kind of a green pill that can affect one's neurological way in a kind that the person can get him deranged out of his sleep.

"What has happened to my father? Answer me, dammit... Nipun! Answer me", Rachel demands from me the situation that has turned her life upside down. She was happy because of her patch up with her love a moment ago, and now her harmony has turned into ruin, but I had to inform her about her father's condition, I couldn't keep this from my best friend, not even after my father commanded me not to reveal the situation to her.

She has obstructed my view of the ground and is standing in front of me. I move my gaze from her feet to her gloomy face. She is about to cry, her eyes are starting to show signs of her doleful soul.

She grabs my shoulders and demands, "Please tell me, Nipun. Why is my father in a sanatorium? What has happened to him?"

"You won't believe me", I say as if I am consoling a crying baby.

"Try me", she prompts.

"Alright... Umm... He found a kind-of green pill somewhere, ate that and fainted. We tried to wake him up, and when he didn't, we went to the hospital. After a week, that was yesterday, he woke up and started babbling about some game, some game of dreams, and said he had to, and kept on saying that. After few hours, he started showing the symptoms of schizophrenia, like, hallucinations including you with a some type of dinosaur and dying; delusions including him asked to murder you; and today, he wasn't even able to think or speak clearly, and...", as I say, she sits on the tree log and starts crying.

I sit beside her and pull her temple to my chest. Her hair smells homey, as if I have been incomplete without her presence.

"He's going to be fine, Raech", I rub her back with my one hand, while my other hand soothes her skull.

I free her from my embrace and she shouts, "No, it's not gonna be fine. You don't know what has happened to him, what he took before... Where is he? I want to meet him".

"Raech, you are not supposed to know about his condition, and not permitted to visit him", I explain calmly.

"Goddammit Nipun. He's my father! I *need* to meet him and you have to take me to him", I can't deny the fact that she loves her father more than anyone in the world, and it's her right to meet him.

I first visited my native sanatorium, Simla Bright Hospital, when I was 13. That experience ended up being my nightmare. It was one of my school's educational trips, I know it sounds weird for a school to be taking children to a sanatorium for education, but our science teacher wanted us to learn about the psychology of people with unstable minds and empathize with them. I heard a rumor that Mrs. Sharma, our science teacher, had a son who grew up being called "crazy", and that's why she decided to revolutionize the Indian society by making them aware of the situation a mental patient goes through and how it is nothing to be made fun of.

We are going from Ward A to Ward B, both having the same structural and interior design, but with the difference of the level of patient's mental disability.

The nurse is staring at Rachel who is rushing behind me, following me to her father. I don't know whether I am doing the right thing by taking her to her father in such a circumstance. The doctor said, hesitating, that Mr. Cox can be recovered if his medication and treatment is regular. The doctor's eyes showed no sign of empathy or sympathy, and I thought this doctor has forgotten about the emotions of his patients by living in midst of the denial of reality.

There he is! Mr. Cox is sleeping under the effect of a strong dose of anesthesia, as prescribed by the Tamil nurse in the morning.

I am standing between the door and the bed as Rachel passes by me. She is staring at her father, when I see one of her tears touching the head of her father. She wipes her face with her hands and kisses Mr. Cox on the same place where her tear found warmth of a good soul.

"I am not leaving him until I talk to him", Rachel says, her eyes fixed on her sleeping muse.

"I am here", this is all I can do right now, support her.

2.

"RACHEL... RUN...", high pitch of Mr. Cox departs Rachel from her sleep, who was sleeping on my shoulder, and makes her run towards him, trying to embrace him with her love; but he doesn't let her touch him.

"I am here dad, I am fine", as Rachel tries to make herself audible to her father, her father was given another injection to stabilize him.

"His situation is getting worse", the nurse looks into my eyes and hustles to her other responsibilities.

As my uncle goes into a deep sleep, Rachel takes the palm of his zombie body, and moves her fingers along his cold bare nerves.

"Rachel?", the woman in black, aunt Katrina, accompanied by my father, enter through the door of despair, "What are you doing here?", to understand what she is saying, you need to be used to her accent.

"Nipun! Did *you* tell her?", my father growls at me.

"I am sorry papa, but she had to know! Nobody but she can heal her father", I explain softly, but before papa could start to say anything else, or rather start to yell, I interfere with his perceptions, "You can't avoid that uncle is calling her name again and again, as if wanting just his daughter and nobody else.

Don't you see that papa?", this time I was empathetic and stern. My words gave him a divine manifestation of realization that I am right in some way, but I know the male ego, he won't accept my tread into his dominating demeanor.

"Go to your home *right now!*", he orders and I step out of the room, waiting for my little friend to sort out her distrust and ambushed feelings.

I have been waiting among the crowd of supporters of their fate, observing the behavior of schizophrenics, rushing nurses, invisible doctors and the family members; some people have hatred for the life they got, while some are just burdened under the responsibilities for their loved ones.

Isn't there any cure for this?

Ward B is the place where you will find social animals grooming to become the part of that world which has decided them to stay in the fantasy world of their minds.

Because of my science teacher, I have studied what a person suffering from schizophrenia goes through, and I have read many biographies, where the victim experiences the hallucinations and delusions of the world of mysterious affairs.

The person suffering is unable to communicate with the outside world, if proper medication is not given, and slowly that person's brain becomes dysfunctional enough to paralyze the senses of the body.

"I can't believe they are doing this to my father", Rachel is standing in front of me, my eyeballs touching my eyelashes, and then shifting to my left as she sits down beside me.

"What are they doing?", I ask.

"They are moving him to an asylum", she answers staring at the grey tiled floor, with her swell red eyes, again inviting the watery glands to secrete some more pain.

She tries to gulp her pain and continues, "We can't let that happen. Nipun?"

"Yes"

"I am going to tell you something, and whether you believe it or not, you will have to trust me on this, will you?", she meets her eyes to mine, and I say, "I trust you!"

She starts her story from the beginning of some dream, which she calls her green dream; she has been a victim of it since her break-up with Erik, the one she used to talk about all the time, some phases included her hatred towards him, while some depicted pure and unconditional love. She tells me about the green pill and some psychologists behind them, the villain of her story, and how they decided to play with the minds of people for their own selfish reasons of experimenting with the God's creations. She tells me the name of the game is Gablet. Then she shortened her story of the five levels she faced, and that to all in her dreams, but with the risk of losing her life in the dream, resulting into the insanity of the person who dies in those dreams. She skips her love rendezvous due to the lack of time and the sensitivity of the situation.

"I want your help to find out who did this to my father", her eyes reflect my need to uncover the secret of the green pill.

"I will do anything I can to help you Raech", as I say this, she hugs and whispers, "Thank you".

3.

We are on a flight to California, where the ratio of foreigners to Asians is 4:6, but I can't see any other Indian. I confess, I am afraid, not because of the game that Rachel told about, but because this is my first time to see Rachel's house. Since all these years, Rachel has always done all the headache of travelling, and I didn't even have the excitement to visit her place.

Since we, Rachel and I, have told our parents about going to California together with the excuse that Rachel can't miss her studies for long, and she wanted me to support her in her dark days, our independent parents permitted us to stay as far away from their problems as much as we can. Rachel called Erik and told him everything about her dad, asking for his directions for reaching the roots of this matter, and she didn't even say 'love you' to him. That's strange!

"Raech?", I interrupt the silence of the cloudy heaven.

She turns to shift her gaze from the clouds below to my ebony eyes, "Yeah?"

"Please don't break again…", it was almost a whisper, and that too, to myself.

"Don't worry, once I find the asshole behind all this, I am going to be normal again!", she replies, and this is the last glib talk happens between us until we reach her house.

California is a very clean city, unlike India; and not only California, but the whole United States of America is beautifully developed. *So this is how it feels in a developed country!* The street where Raech is living, what was the name… has large houses with large gardens, and Raech told me once that there is a swimming pool as well, and I was like 'wow… I envy you'.

Erik was already waiting for her arrival on the porch of her house. She jumps on him to hug him and whispers something in his ears. Whilst their romance, I observe the huge garden in front of the porch. *I didn't know she was that rich!* And when I turn towards the alienated street, I feel like my heart and mind have been controlled by the peace of this new era of silence.

Why didn't I come here before?

"Nipun, this is Erik", Rachel pulls my concentration to another American, he offers to shake his hand, "Erik, Nipun", as Rachel chops the air from my direction to his and again to mine, I take Erik's hand with a compliment, "Nice to, finally, meet you".

"Same here", I reply with a small grin.

"You are a lucky guy", I say, and as we grace each other with Rachel's kind and lively belongingness, Rachel enters to meet her bitch and temporarily forgets about the two guys waiting to rescue her from her pain.

She clears her black sofa, hides some kind of a diary covered in brown, and beckons us to sit.

The sullen sofa is sitting side-faced with the entrance door, talking with the TV and a center table providing them an ease for their engagement.

Erik and I are occupying each corner of the sofa, while Raech has pulled a chair in front of us, forming a triangle of suspense.

The common node initiates, "Erik, from where did you find that green pill?"

"My younger brother's bag. I recently found out that every child of his class gets the same pill once a day, but he never told me anything about this before. When I asked him the reaction of the pill, he just said he didn't remember. He said, he was supposed to gulp it in the class, but because of cough, he put it aside and his teacher didn't notice, so he got out with this indiscipline", Erik explains.

How come he knew all this and didn't tell Rachel before? And how come his brother and the school got involved? Something isn't right!

Meanwhile, Rachel got drifted to the understanding of Erik's words, or say, fantasy story.

"Raech, can I talk to you in private for a moment?", I ask Rachel. She takes a quick glance at Erik and walks with me towards the kitchen.

"Don't you feel something's wrong with that story? I mean, how come he is telling you about that school now? And if his brother has been taking that pill, then how come his parents haven't taken any step by now? And if his brother's whole class has been taking it, then how come they are sane till now?", I try to open up her eyes and create suspicion to the trivial details of the delusional story.

Rachel gives my words a thought for a minute, sighs and replies, "I know you won't be believing almost anything of what is just happening, but you need to trust me".

"I trust you Raech, I just don't trust what Erik said out there", I say, calmly, waving my hands in front of me, they are acting as my communicator.

"Sonu, I trust him more than myself, and I *need* you to trust him. Will you do that for me?", she has adorable eyes, and I can't refuse anything to those brown eyes; they look at me as if longing for me to stay with them, forever.

I nod, and we head to the living room. Erik is sitting with both of his elbows meeting his respected knees, and his hands gripping his hair, tight, as if wanting to pull out his brain.

You might trust him Raech, but I can never trust him!

4.

When I had the fortune of my mother making my bed and singing me to sleep, I had a best friend in my school, named ShivamKhandelwal. I remember that name from the core of my heart, since he stabbed my heart until it bled dry. I used to tell him everything about me, and vice versa, or so I thought.

When we were in class 5, the heavenly bodies sent to our class a girl with extravagant sweetness; she joined our class and was given the seat right in front of ours. I knew that Shivam, too, had a huge crush on her, but what I didn't know was he would play a dirty game with me to get her.

Since I used to tell him my every little secret, I told him that I fantasized about making-out with my neighbor. This might not seem a big deal, but in India, it is a mark of having a bad child in the society. Shivam exaggerated this thing and told Sadhvi, our crush, and the whole class, that I had done much more than just fantasizing and I had been watching porn since a month. He not only played this dirty little trick for just getting a girl, but he also forced me into writing a love letter and then he edited it, adding dirty things like kissing and sex fantasies and passed it on to the principal, resulting in an embarrassed year at the school.

I was a child then, and I didn't reckon the two-sided faces of humans, but when one of my classmates told me about my little secret revealed by my so-called "best friend", I learned the consequence of trusting people in a blink of an eye; and since this affected my child-heart, I have never been able to trust anyone easily again.

5.

While Erik has been reciting his side of story of Gablet, I have been scrutinizing his body language, trying to find any sign of defiance or betrayal; like for example, I read a book on body language that depicted the hidden meanings of the body movements. When someone gestures through his forehand, or palm, that someone is telling the truth; or the number of times that someone blinks eyes is also related to the true or false prediction of that someone; and the most expressive part of the body is the pair of legs, since toes and ankles are the farthest from human sight, humans forget to take control over their toes, and the direction of the toes reveal the truth of what that someone is actually up to.

Based on many more studies on body language, I am trying to study Erik's mind. His toes are pointing towards Raech, his hands' gestures are honest, his posture seems neutrally inclined, but his eyes say different, as if they are hiding some part of an equation to solve the mystery of the game of dreams, or to revert Uncle Jack Cox to his normal self.

The story ends with their romance after about half an hour, where he told about his first stage including chiliad lizards, his second stage reverting to the time spent with Rachel and his fear of losing her (I rolled my eyes), his third stage being in the forest in midst of his house in London, his fourth stage where the past of his grandmother's death was unleashed, and the fifth stage being the common one for both Raech and him; and I skipped all the details since I found them a waste of time.

"Can we concentrate on finding the antidote to your father's insanity instead?", I interrupt their rubbish talk.

"We are trying to do that only. I told my story to find any hidden clue in the games and to match any of Raech's story to find any pattern in all these dreams", Erik replies.

I nod, staring at his hazel green eyes. One of my friends once told me that people with hazel eyes should not be trusted in their talks, and this seems one more reason for me to not to trust him.

"So, what we need to do is, first, find the supplier", Erik's gaze is constant on Rachel, "and there is only one pattern to all the dreams, as the level increases, the depth of your inner soul comes forward and you are forced to live in it".

"Nicely said", I compliment.

He glances at me and, again, continues to stare at Rachel, waiting for her reaction.

"Let's find your brother's teacher then", she replies, completely trusting the guy with the hazel green eyes sitting in front of her. She turns towards me and asks, "Are you with me?"

"Yes. That's why I came here, to save your dad, didn't I?", I am disappointed that she has to even ask that question, I will always be with her, no matter how much I distrust the people around her.

She smiles, "I know…", and the smile fades, "I am sorry."

"We should get some food and rest and continue our investigation tomorrow", Erik interrupts.

Rachel turns towards him and replies, "Let's eat some food and get going with the search. I can't afford to lose another day with my father in that condition".

He nods and starts towards the door. He is standing at the entrance, poised to move away from Lindsey. Rachel kisses Lindsey goodbye, calls Lindsey's caretaker, feeds her bitch food and water and while slamming the door close, shouts her comeback.

After having lunch, we are standing in front of a school. It is almost 5 in the evening according to California time zone, and almost 5.30 in the morning of the next day in my hometown.

Our walk towards the school was awkward, mostly for Rachel. She sensed that Erik and I are not getting along, so she decided to either talk about solving the mystery of the green pill, or choosing the side of silence and peaceful walk; but mostly her face showed worry for her father. In between, I tried to hold her hand and express that Uncle Cox will be fine, but instead Erik reached for her other hand, as Raech was in between, and they started their romantic talks for a while. I am happy if she is happy, but I need to prove Erik's innocence and true love in my eyes.

I remember the time when Erik left Raech and her heart died from the pain that she used to suppress every single moment. I knew she cried every night, she didn't tell me anything about it, and my admiration for her grew from a plant to a tree and I realized that my best friend is the strongest person in the world, and that's why I am giving a chance to Erik, because Raech trusts him.

The school in front of us has Japanese edifice.

"Erik, why is your brother's school Japanese?", Rachel's healthy mind asks Erik.

"Yeah… I never mentioned this to you. My brother is Japanese", he replies, his teeth talking the weirdness of the situation and his lips stretched as if guilty for hiding a huge secret, "He is adopted".

As Erik explains the questioning pair of eyes, both Raech and I have our wide eyes trying to penetrate into Erik's adopted Japanese brother's story; but Rachel might have realized about her father waiting for her in an asylum, shouting her name and a way to escape his miserable life, and she continues her

journey towards the inside of the Brown and Red
Japanese hatted school of Erik's brother.

6.

I never had a long relationship, or a real girlfriend. Some came in my life to prove to me why trust is a sin, and others taught me how love can be just an interpretation of one's mind, rather than of heart. Rachel has been always there for me, whether it has been my sin or sane.

My friends used to tease me of my relationship with Rachel, but deep in my heart, I always knew that I won't dare ruin our friendship with any kind of intimate love; and in the end, you need a true friend in your bad times.

When you look inside your heart, you feel a large hole formed by the missing mirth in the form of living being, and when that being reverts in your life, an even larger hole is created for the ordeal of more love. I have been feeling the same since I was 13. I was entranced by my first love, Romita.

Romita was nicknamed as 'the black one' by our schoolmates, because of her dark complexion, but for me, she was the pilot of her dreams. I flew with her in her dreams in her first conversation. My heart broke its vow of silence and convinced me that she had a heart of a holy bird. She wanted to soar to the outermost virtual eccentric circle representing the Earth. She is the most ambitious girl I have ever met, and this attracted me towards her. I was her second priority, her first being her passion for heights and flying, and I presumed that she left the school to be a part of the flying schools. Apart from her ambitious charisma, I fell in love with her shiny black eyes, like mine, as charming as a *kancha*, played to take someone else's place.

She always used to say, "I am meant to touch the sky, and the sky is limitless for me", and I used to gaze straight through her eyes with amazement getting the reflection of her dazzling dreams.

I fell in love with her even though I knew that she was meant to marry the sky and not a limited soul, and so I decided to let her go of my feelings in the air with her.

Why am I remembering my past with Romita all of a sudden? That's because I am standing in front of her right now. Curly hair, dull dark skin, horn-rimmed glasses, white shirt and blue skirt; her alien eyes penetrating through mine, trying to find the existence of reality of my presence and her mind looking for the reason of the elliptical nature of the world. What I can see in her eyes is numbness; no dreams, no light and no life, just emptiness.

"Romita?", I jump out of my chosen adventure and walk towards her, leaving the untrustworthy boyfriend and my best friend astounded, behind me, inside the Japanese wooden aged classroom of Erik's younger brother, Riku.

Tears start rolling from her eyes, touching the still golden smile of hers. She is standing frozen in front of me, captured by evil power of memories and emotions. She cannot believe my presence at this moment. Trapped by her darkness for a long time, she had lost all her hope for the light of freedom.

I expect her to jump towards me and hug me, but all she does is stand numb. *My complexion is not that dark that she can't even distinguish me from my surroundings.* She is held by an invisible harness. I step forward to reach her hands. Her smile vanishes and all that she is left with are her tears of a prisoner.

I hug her and whisper in her black open hair, "I can save you".

She detaches herself from me, looks me in my eyes, looking for the secret she has been hiding from the world, then hugs me back, desperate for love and affection.

In the midst of her mitigated sobs, she replies, "You shouldn't be here. Go back to India. You don't belong here".

"Neither do you", I pull myself away to swallow the pain in the strong-willed pair of eyes.

"What are you doing here?", I break the ice of silence, "You were supposed to be fulfilling your dreams of being the world's best female pilot".

With this sentence, she gives up and a gush of tears start flowing from her helpless eyes. She turns her back towards me, and I observe a dozen children in the room, gazing at their school teacher's unexpected change of emotions. One of those kids is looking behind me instead of the crying black beauty.

Erik beckons that kid, and the kid flies towards the elder guardian. Erik sits on his knees and whispers to the kid, "We need to go right now. Do you understand?"

Riku nods and both of them leave the Japanese ambience, leaving behind Rachel, who is waiting for me to join the journey of saving her father.

"You need to come with me", my firm voice calls to Romita.

"No! You should leave", she replies, facing the children.

I take grasp of her arm, moving towards the exit as one. She doesn't even try to resist my action.

7.

"What are you doing here? Why are you teaching a bunch of Japanese kids? You should be up there", I point my index finger to the sky, my pupils peeking at the highest range above me, "penetrating through the clouds, touching your dreams in this divine universe. What are you doing *here*?", I ask her as we reach the end of the road of the Japanese school.

She is staring at me. Soft eyes, subtle face, child-like innocence that wants me to decipher her restraints and show me her plights. She might be imagining a magical touch that can make me feel what she has felt. Her lips shut tightly in the grimness of her past.

"Nipun?", she calls with all my attention to her. I am willing to give all my time in listening to her journey to California, and I am longing for her carefree smile, "I don't need your help. Just go and leave me alone!"

She doesn't move a muscle, and neither do I. Her mind might want me to stay distant, but I know that her heart is desperate for my protective shell. This strong girl is asking me to leave her behind in her own ordeal, but I made a promise to myself, and my principles have higher priority than my personal life.

Ignoring her denial to talk, I ask her, "Do you know anything about… umm… Raech? What was…", I ask for help.

"Gablet", the silence of a broken and desperate heart breaks through the light of hope when Rachel replies to me.

Romita's face becomes paler, as if Rachel has foretold her death. "How do you know that name?", she jumps out of her misery.

I explain the long story in 3 minutes and 20 seconds, ending the true tale with the same question as before, "What are you doing here?"

"Oh shit!", her eyes fall to the ground, "I didn't know this would go this far. How many lives have been taken?"

"Taken? None that we know of. Became insane… my father and God knows how many else", Rachel replies.

Romita's eyes strike at the existence of Riku, clutching the hand of his elder step brother, and she shouts, "Go back to your classroom".

Riku, scared, looks up at his brother's angry face, expecting him for throwing a shield in front of Riku.

"He will stay with me", Erik orders firmer than Romita, his green eyes vividly transforming into a guardian.

"You don't understand", Romita's voice softens, "He *needs* to be in the classroom. Otherwise he..."

"Otherwise what?"

"Otherwise..."

BOOM!

8.

I am lying and circling. I can't decipher whether it's my head, or if the ground is spinning, or is it both. I try to open my eyes, but an external force is pushing my eyelids back to the dizzy darkness. I feel as if I have been beaten a million times and then thrown at a revolving ground.

After my best efforts, I move one of my fingers, my ring finger. When I become capable of observing the depth of this 3D world, I feel dizzy, and as if I am revolving.

"Nipun… Nipun? Wake up, Nipun", my ears filter these words from between the drum rolls playing in the arena of the real world. "We need to go. Get up, Nipun", a hand feathers my shoulder, leaving me painless and fulfilling my destiny of meeting the Goddess of love.

"Aah…", I screech out of the pain in my balls. That lover has kicked on my nuts.

"I am sorry Nipun, but we need to leave *now*", her voice reaches a recognizable state, and my vision gradually makes sense out of the dark skin provoking my wheatish skin to save our lives.

The pain between my legs is excruciating, numbing the other damaged parts of my body, concentrating all my senses to just the one part.

"Come on Nipun, *get up*", the Goddess of love has now turned into a nemesis as I follow her devilish voice.

I keep my hands steady, legs together and pull myself up from a red circular spinning bed. *Where am I?*

Romita grabs my right arm and almost drags me from the tall bed to the underground. "From where do you girls find so much power?", I manage to ask.

"From our hearts! Now get moving, Nipun", one Indian yells to another Indian, "Those children got roasted in the fire, and you are just complaining about your energy".

Her words crawl through my ears and reach every one of my vein, artery, blood cell and then my heart and mind, until I remember everything happened outside that Japanese school. My past replays in front of me...

"You don't understand. He needs to be in the classroom. Otherwise he...",Romita stammered.

"Otherwise what?", Erik asked.

"Otherwise...", and the school danced into flames, transforming itself into ashes of memories of the lost children. The orange-red colored school was forfeited by the same but intensified colors of death and life. My world was overtaken by the sound of silence and the burning heat. The flames were so zealous that they dominated the gravity, making us fly, only to get us slapped by the karma of the ground; and in the air, the grey ghostly blanket entrapped our breathes, until the dark shadow ate all five of us.

"Oh my God", I blurt with my wide eyes, "How many children were in there?", I am almost on my legs, my inner power taking over my external one.

"I don't know", she replies, searching for an exile out of this emotional derangement.

We peek from our white-colored door for any sign of fatality, but all we encounter is silence.

"Where are Rachel and Erik?", my best friend can be seen nowhere. How can I be oblivious about it!

"Might be in the other room", she replies, distracted by her stealth, "Let's get out of here while we still have a chance". She clutches my arm and nearly drags me, again, out of the love-making room to a white corridor. As I follow her sneaky steps, I observe scorched dorsal-side of her right hand. I move my thumb across her right hand, as she is leading me towards safety. She glances at my smoothening thumb and then at me, with her eyes begging me to rescue her from pain in the cage of dreams.

"How did you get this?", I ask.

"During the school blast, I guess", she replies in a professional tone.

"Isn't this hurting you?", I ask.

"No. I am not allowed to feel pain", she replies.

"What do you mean you are not *allowed* to? We don't have to ask for permission to feel pain", I give an obvious remark.

She doesn't answer.

"Sonu!", I look back at my best friend. She leaves Erik's hand and hugs me, "I am glad you're okay". Her face brightens on my sight. I smile back and she returns to Erik's intimacy. I analyze her from top to bottom, and she hasn't got a scratch.

"You look at peace!", I am surprised of her sudden change of heart.

"Yeah", she glances at Erik, "My father has been cured", her white teeth joins the glamor of her white skin.

"How?", my smile vanishes with the inception of suspicion.

"I don't know that; but I saw a dream", she replies, "In my dream, he was asking me to come home and he said that he has been given the right treatment out of the insanity", she continues to smile, "We need to go home, Nipun. It's over. He's fine. Everything's fine now".

"Raech... How can you blindly believe your dream? It was *just* a *dream*", I see my index finger in front of me, strongly pointing at her to question her absurdness.

"Gablet, too, was a dream, Nipun, still it was real to our minds. I can feel my father", she looks at me, waiting for a support, but when she doesn't get any, she continues, "Can you just trust me and support me on this?"

I can't nod this time. I can't support her this time. I sense something's out of the pattern here, someone's playing with her mind, manipulating her like a puppeteer, but still I can't break her heart, and I nod unwillingly. I lie to her because I can't see her gloomy side again.

Her smile returns, as if her whole life was dependent on my support, "Okay! So let's get home".

9.

"Mum"

"Mum?"

"Don't leave me, mum. Please don't leave me. I will explain the whole society. You don't have to leave for them. Please don't leave me alone like this!"

"Mummy, NO", I helplessly bellow, as she jumps in the well.

I jerk my way up on the bed, breaking my sleep through my naïve tears filled in my eyes. I never let them fall down, because I don't want myself to feel weak. The dream with my mother killing herself, haunts me, leaving me empty from inside. I feel guilt, guilt of not being able to save my mother, guilt of still living in a society that is oblivious about emotions, and all they are interested in gossiping and interfering in other's lives.

"I am sorry, mum", I say and start to cry like a baby. Someone comes in my intimacy and hugs me, saying, "It's fine, Nipun. It was just a dream".

For a moment, I continue to cry in the arms of an unknown fairy, but then I get back to the reality, "Who are you?", I cringe backwards.

From the darkness of my past, a melodious voice pulls me to the present, "It'sRaech, Sonu".

In the darkness, I can't see her face, but I can feel her. I move my hands across her face, trying to capture the structure of her face in my soul. From her glossy hair covering her eyes, to her pointed nose, to her juicy lips, to her shoulder, and I am convinced of my eternal feelings.

"Where are we?", I ask, cupping my hands to her chin, as if praying together for our release.

"I don't know. We are lost in the factory of those maddening green pills", she replies, trying to find light in her dark path.

"What about getting home to your father? Didn't you say that he was healed?", I ask as I follow her steps away from the bed to the black alley.

"I lied", she tightens the grip of her hand. She is afraid of something.

"But why?"

"Romita is one of them."

My step freezes at the mention of Romita, "One of them? Who is *them*?"

"The psychologists! They created that green pill, and they are the reason for Gablet to rule over people's minds. They are the culprits of my father's insanity", she replies, and even in this indistinct blackness, I can see rage in her eyes.

"How can you say that she's one of them?", I ask, my heartbeat getting faster and louder.

"When the school went aflame, everyone went unconscious, except Romita and I, but she didn't realize that I was watching her the whole time. She dragged us to this place and told her seniors to finish us off. But her emotions overruled her mind, and she couldn't kill you, so she tried to hypnotize you with those same pills. Till she could get hold of that pill, Erik and I came in her way and she tried to convince us that she was trying to save us. When Erik and I met you in that white corridor, your mind was already a little bit in her influence, so I decided to outsmart her and tied her in a room. Remember Erik taking Romita with her? Erik is taking care of her, and we need to find that antidote now and get the hell out of here", she stops, "I don't know where we are heading to!"

"Okay…", I try to digest everything that my oldest friend briefed me about. *Romita can't hurt anyone. I know her.*

"Where has Erik taken Romita?", I ask Rachel as she tries to decipher her way ahead.

"I don't know. He was moving ahead of me, and then the lights went off, and now we are here, lost".

"How did I fall asleep?", I ask.

"I hit you on the back, and was dragging you all the way on the gurney", she replies.

I touch at my swollen skull, "Ouch…"

"Sorry, Sonu, but I had to do that, otherwise Romita wouldn't have left you alone", she whispers.

I take a deep breath and the sound of my exhaling echoes, "Raech?"

"Hm?"

"We need to wait for the lights."

"We can't wait, Nipun. We need to find that antidote and cure my father. We can't waste our time *here*", her voice is desperate and in vain.

I grab her shoulder and strongly reply, "We can't move until and unless we don't see anything. Try to understand, Raech. What if we bump into one of those psychologists? We need to hide somewhere until the light comes. Do you understand?"

"Hm", she mumbles.

We wave our hands in front of us, trying to find a place to ambush. There's a door on our left. We enter into another darkness of compactness, and we sit under a table, waiting to be rescued from this unknown disaster.

After 5 minutes, I break the ice cold silence, "Raech?"

"Hm?"

"You have changed."

After a minute or two that felt like eternity, she replies, "I know."

Her face under the table in the small cabinet lit up as light shows its way to our dark world. We peek to the outer world through the door. Rachel can't wait to find the antidote and go back to her father. The white corridor is gone, welcoming a crowded work area. There are white people running from east to west and vice versa with a pin drop silence. It seems like a hospital by observing their attire.

"Grab a uniform and ride along", Rachel orders.

I look backwards and there is a bundle of green uniforms hanging from a trolley. We pick one each and slide it over our current clothing.

I follow Raech out of the room and reach in the midst of a portable crowd of white people. *How can I ride along white people with a different skin color?*

It seems these busy people don't care who they are walking along with. It's like an army of busy white ants working day and night for their survival. *Why are they working like machines?*

A lady with blonde hair crosses me, her eyes crystal blue, and focused on her path, unknown of her surroundings. A man almost ran past me, expressionless, crystal green eyes.

"Sonu, peek through all the doors in the way, we need to find the leader of these psychologists", she says in a single breath, molded like a machine, like others.

I follow my comrade in the crowd of unknown, only to get lost in the crowd of educated puppets.

As we pass through different doors with no labels, I stop, clutch Rachel's arm, making her rotate towards me, waving her golden hair from her back to her front, "Look", I point.

We gasp at the disgust of the sight. Raech opens the door with her right hand and we freeze on the sight of the blanket of cruelty covered by the humans and the dusk of new era of Hitler.

The rows of cages are holding every type of animal, and all of them are as silent as a grave. I have seen many types of animal experimentations, a.k.a. animal cruelty, in movies, but I haven't seen the experimented animals silent, rather they become violent after being treated as human's objects. They should be shouting for their freedom, but this case is the opposite. Here, they seem like they are dreaming in another dimension. All of them have their gazes fixed on our steps forward, as if amazed by the structure of humans. Gorilla, Bonobo, Orangutan, Lion, Tiger, Cheetah, Vulture, Eagle, Chipmunk, Sloth, Rabbit, Cat, Dog; name the animal and it's here. Every type of reptile, rodent, mammal or bird caged solo, as if a curious child collecting different animal toys aiming for the trophy of a diversified animal collector.

I scrutinize from one type of animal to another and then my eyes freeze on Rachel. She has tears in her eyes that are about to kiss her left cheek. She is extremely compassionate towards animals, and watching them in this condition treated like objects kept in a museum named 'Zombie Animals', might have broken her strong and sensitive heart.

I interlock my hand with hers. She responds, "I am going to cure them and free them, no matter what!"

Her conviction towards animal savory is what has changed my perceptions. I have respected her and her compassion from the day I first met her.

"*We* are going to rescue them", I reply.

She untangles our hands and points towards the far-end of the animal slavery laboratory, "Look there's someone".

As the animals quietly focus on our movements, with stealth, we move towards the ajar door, light showing its way from below, showing its way to the darkness of the aisle of dawn of insanity.

I follow Rachel, instead of the other way around. I should be protecting her. She asks for a knife, or any other fatal tool. I look around and find some chemicals arranged for experimentations. I beckon Rachel to wait at her current position, and I move towards the little laboratory to read the names of the different chemicals.

Here it is! I pick up a flask labelled, 'Sulphurous Acid', and walk in front of Rachel, guarding her from the unknown peril.

When we reach the door, we sneak in to find Erik rummaging the cabinet, with papers lying on the floor, files opened, and drawers and cupboards showing their inner wealth.

"Oh my God. Erik, it's you", she runs towards him and jumps on him to hug him, "I was insanely worried about you. Thank God you are fine", she kisses him on his lips, like a small tap from a lip to another lip.

"I knew you would be safe with Nipun though", he glances at me, without a smile. It doesn't seem that he is grateful of me.

I return his look with a confused one.

"I know who did this to your father", Erik's eyes are fixed on Rachel, both of his hands on her shoulder.

Rachel's emotions quietens her, she is taking her time to let the suspense reach her veins and wrestle with her vocal chords for any vibration.

"It's his father", he points his index finger right at me.

Rachel's eyes follow that index finger. She is deciding her next step, looking for the right in wrong and wrong in right.

"His father is the creator of that green pill, and your father", he turns back to face Rachel, "might have found out", and then back to me, "so his father might have decided to send your father to the world of insanity".

"No", this is all Raech could exhale.

She is begging for answers through her eyes, her gaze following my eye movements. When her patience wears out, she asks, "Say something, Nipun! Tell me that Erik's wrong. I am sure there's an explanation".

I look in her eyes bewildered, and marooned from the capability of understanding the emotions of human beings.

"He's correct", I respond.

She wobbles backwards, opting for the support of the wooden table that has witnessed the truth from the inception of the creation of sanity to its end.

"I didn't know about the green pill before papa gave it to Mr. Cox. Believe me, Raech. I knew nothing of his work", I explain, helping her to join the dots of an unending puzzle.

"You mean to say that your father travelled up and down India and California and you or your mother didn't even suspect anything?", Erik asks sarcastically.

On the word 'mother', my expression went from explanatory to gloomy. Rachel senses this and softly interrupts my past tragedy, "Why did you do this, Nipun?"

"I was trying to help you, Raech. At least *you* should believe me. You are my childhood friend, I can *never* betray you. *Never,*Raech!", my eyes fill with tears of fear of losing my one and only best friend.

"How were you helping me?", she replies.

"I was making sure that you follow the right path to finding the antidote. *I* made sure that you find *this* place", I clarify.

"*Romita* brought us here, not *you*", Rachel's eyes fill with tears of anger.

"*I* told Romita to do whatever she did; and now she is in danger. I need to go and help her", I reply with concern for both of my childhood friends.

"I don't want to waste any more time in arguing about the truth. Can you help me find that antidote?", she asks, without looking for further explanations of my honesty. I don't know if she trusts me or if her mind is tethered by the burden of curing her father.

"I don't know where it is in this laboratory", I answer disappointed with myself.

"Bullshit! He is lying, Raech", Erik prompts.

"I am not! I came this far for finding that only. You have to believe me, Raech. I would never do anything to hurt you", my devastation turns into a firm and confident reply.

"If you really want to help, call up and ask your father to get that antidote", Erik says.

"I would have done this on the first place if this would have been that easy. He doesn't know that I know about Gablet, and he can't ever know this, otherwise I don't know if I will survive in his world or not", I reply.

"I have a plan", smiles Rachel.

10.

"How's my father, uncle?", Rachel asks.

"In the same condition as you left him, Rachel. I am sorry", Mr. Della replies through the speaker of his iPhone.

Rachel roll her eyes and continues, "Uncle, I called you because there's an emergency. It's about your son".

We sense my father's worry as he asks, "Is he alright?"

"No, uncle. He too has taken the green pill, and he is unconscious. I have already tried everything to wake him up, but he doesn't seem to move even an inch", I try to act worried and confused.

"I am on my way to California", he has accepted the bait.

While we wait for his return, we brace for our next plan at Rachel's house.

"I wish my father was here to guide me", Rachel says as the three musketeers on the couch with Rachel bridging the 2 poles of her life.

Before I could reply, Erik takes hold of her hands and says, "That time is not far". Rachel smiles, and kisses him on his lips.

"Raech, I am sleepy. Where can I rest?", I ask, realizing the need to provide the reunited couple a far-from-the-world time.

"Feel free to rest in my room. It is the first room to the right upstairs", she replies.

I follow her instruction and take the stairs, where I bump into her family photographs hanging on the wall on my way to upstairs. First photo is of Rachel's bitch, Lindsey. When she bought Lindsey with her, she recited every single detail of how that Beagle bathed, ate, wagged her tail, jumped on her; Lindsey was Rachel's only unconditional love back then.

In the photo, Lindsey is drooling at the sight of the cameraman, and her eyes look more innocent than a human baby's, as if asking for something, might be food, or love.

The next photo consists of Lindsey with Rachel. Rachel is hugging her bitch, and her bitch is looking away from the camera. Almost every dog does that. They are not even a bit interested in posing for a snap.

The next photo consists of the photo of her parents and brother, accompanied by an angry Rachel without her bitch.

"You should be nice to him. He's my childhood best friend", I listen to a muffled voice of a girl.

"I don't know why, but I am unable to develop trust for him", Erik replies, in a voice that I have never heard of him, a seductive voice.

"Trust him for my sake, Erik. Will you?", she asks.

"On one condition, if you kiss me like I am the last man left on the Earth", Erik replies, and their doggo conversation transformed into the desire for love.

I almost stumble on the last stair. I turn right and enter in the first dark room of my life. I mean literally. It is painted black.

Why her room is painted black?

My pathfinder being the effulgent welcomed by the glass window, I move across the room decorated with varied sketches in white.

The black wall facing her bed has a horse embraced to another by their necks, bringing light and warmth to the black background.

Following is her 'TO DO LIST' written on the right side of the wall.

> TO DO:
>
> Buy Lindsey food
>
> Complete assignment
>
> Find an apartment

Buy groceries

I move back to her bed covered by a black bed sheet. I knew that she is in love with the color black, but I didn't know that she is obsessed with it.

I fall backwards to the bed. The ceiling is designed in the shape of a full moon.

I crawl back till my head finds the pillow and think about the crazy minds of human beings.

Sometimes, I imagine a world where humans are labeled with their pros and cons floating above their heads. When I would meet anybody, I would know whom to send in jail, and whom to teach about the natural world.

I am obsessed with psychology. How human brains react on different emotions! How one can manipulate other's emotions and decisions! The functionalities of a mind intrigue me, magnetizing me into a world where I would have the power to lay open a human's mind and learn everything there is to learn. Labelling them would make it recklessly easy and hence make human's lives easier, which is good in its own way. Still, humans demand complications, so that they find a firm reason to carry on their lives.

Then I fall into a sound sleep.

"Mum, NO!", I am standing inside an old barn. My mother is a feet away from the portentous deep well. I bellow her to live, for her return. I try to run to her and save her, but I am mentally tethered at my place, unable to move even by an inch. She doesn't look back and jumps to the devil of death.

With my open eyes, I sit straight, "Mum, NO!", the exact words come from my Adam's apple that I used before my mum jumped 14 years ago.

I seek for water, following the steps in reverse that I drew for reaching Rachel's room. With stealth, I try not to disturb the two lovers sleeping one over the other, naked under the blanket. I reach the kitchen, open the refrigerator door, drink water and head back to the black hole.

I rewind my plan over and over till my sleep gets me and makes love to me.

11.

"Nipun? Nipun? NIPUN!", I wake up to the effulgent afternoon with Rachel's charming face in front of me, calling for me.

"Nipun, your father has reached California and now he is on his way here. What you got to do is act asleep as if you are never gonna wake up! God forbid. At that time, I will ask him about the antidote", she says, keeping my brunch, an omelet and a cup of coffee at my bedside.

"No, Raech. I have a better plan. Trust me on this. I need you to stay down and wait for me", I sit up facing her innocent brown eyes. Her eyes are gleaming at me, showing her joyous sleepy eyes. She didn't sleep properly the night before.

"What do you mean? You don't know how that green pill works", she replies.

"I have been a great observer of Mr. Cox. Believe me, I know what I am doing. I will get your antidote, Raech, no matter what it takes!," I hold her hand and squeeze it, waiting for her nod.

After a minute's silence, she nods.

I smile and take the command, "Now go downstairs and prepare to bring the fool out of papa".

She gets to the door, gives me a last glance of trustworthy suspicion and heads downwards.

I have my brunch, lay back in the light reflected from the darkness of the room and wait for the villain of the story.

"Nipun? Nipun! Wake up, Sonu. I am here. Papa has come to you. Please say something!", papa has come to save me. With my closed eyes, I can imagine his pretentious worried face, while his hands run from my head to neck, checking out my temperature and pulse. He has developed a polymath in him all these years.

While he turns his head towards Rachel, I peek and beckon her to leave the room.

"I don't know why he isn't waking up. You should continue to talk to him. I am gonna go and bring water", she replies, glancing at my waving hands.

Her canny mind has always attracted me towards her. While she excuses herself and closes the door behind her, papa continues to babble about his love for me, my value in his life, calling me back from my deep sleep, and other pathetic sentimental stuff.

"Drawer… Drawer… Drawer…", I whisper, predicting him to follow my clue.

He replies with, "Drawer? Where? Here? Wait! I am opening it. What now? Tell me, *beta*. What now?"

"Eat the green pill", I do as I have been planning for years. With my closed eyes, I say these words, perfectly framed and practiced almost a million times, audible enough only to my so-called "papa", and whispering in my sleep. He doesn't understand the pattern of reality, what he understands are the words of society and voice of critics.

"Ok. I am taking the pill. I will do whatever it takes for me to recover you. I am taking the pill", in my blindness, my hearing power becomes stronger, capable to make alive his each step. His last words are followed by the thump on the floor near the bedside. He is gone into a long unbreakable sleep. He is gone to another game of dreams. Gone to *his* dreadful fears. I want him to feel every bit of pain my mother experienced only because of him. I want him to live my moments of emptiness, when I needed my mother the most, and she was in the heaven only because of him.

I have fulfilled my destiny. I have avenged the death of mum. She might have had an extra-marital affair, but she was my mother *and* his wife. He didn't even bother to ask the reason for her betrayal. He could have asked about her circumstances; why did she betray him? She might have fallen in love with someone else. He might not have treated her well. Love doesn't knock one's door before coming. He could have reasoned with her and sorted things out; but instead, he chose to listen to the society's sarcasm. He was worried that the society will call him insane. Well, his worst nightmare is gonna come true, he has become truly insane now.

I smile as I see his asleep face lying on the floor in front of me. An asleep helpless face. He has destroyed my life. He is the reason of my mum's death. He is the reason of my loneliness. The reason for an emptiness that has consumed my childhood. I couldn't stand to see him happy while my heart ached. Every single time he laughed, I felt my heart twitching and tearing apart a little bit more. His time for laying down and introspecting has come. He needs to look inside himself long and deep before being able to judge and control other people's lives.

I pull him on the bed, with difficulty, and sit beside him, scrutinizing his breathing chest. His wrinkled skin is reflecting his fears. Those glowing ebony eyes are, now, laying shut to brace him for his crazy future. His clothes are clean and ironed, reflecting his persnickety side of life.

I could have murdered him, if I didn't get the opportunity to make that green pill useful.

I run my hand in my right pocket of my jeans and stare at the blue pill in between the ups and downs of my palm, balanced by the gravity.

I walk downstairs, innocent and a savior.

"Are you alright?", Rachel runs towards me and hugs me.

"Never better", I give a big shining smile, exposing the antidote covered in blue color.

"Is this…", she is interfered by me, "The life jacket of your drowning father".

She kisses me on my left cheek and shows her gratification. Her hair caresses my nose, and parts its essence after kissing my lips.

"We need to fly to my dad immediately", she glows under the light of faith.

"I need to stay here with my father", I reply. The word *papa* has lost its value for me.

"What are you going to do? How have you taken this pill from him? How…", I block her way to upstairs.

"I need you to trust me and go to your father with Erik. Take care of your father, and I will take care of mine here. Erik, take her", I command.

"But you don't even know the roads here", she replies, her forehead furrowed.

"I will manage, Raech. Trust me!", I hold her hands and see right through her sparkling brown eyes, she trusts me. "You need to go to your father. Now!"

My words break her glass of confusion. She refuses to leave me alone in this foreign land, but when Erik and I convince her about the better of her father, she follows my lead, gives me instructions about Lindsey's timely meals and other household needs, grabs her already-packed luggage and she assures her return as soon as her dad returns to the world of sanity.

I continue to nod as I follow her through the house and she explains the pedantic necessities moving out from her living room. She hugs me, kisses Lindsey and bids worried and glorious farewell to us. She is, now, on her way to the end of an adventure named as the game of dreams.

12.

I free myself from my pretentious self. My heart has blackened over time. I take out my phone, and let my dial pad become useful, "It's done". Now, it's my waiting time.

I replace Lindsey's water, add some more dog food in her bowl, caress her and lie on the sofa, thinking about Rachel. She has been my best friend since my childhood. She has been always there for me whenever I needed her. All I needed to do was to call her, and she would answer me with her lively self.

I have been played by many people, used by my buddies, and when I came to the realization of my trust and love for Rachel, she had left for California. I am desperate to tell her how I feel for her. I understand that she has Erik in her life as her "boyfriend", but I have sensed a stronger feeling for me from her side. She might not love me the way I do, but I am positive that she loves me.

I go in my past to see her smile, her mischievous eyes, her childish cheeks, her deep heart and her pure soul. All I need to do is make her realize her love for me, and then I am 100% sure that she will leave Erik for me.

I switch on the TV and continue to surf channels, until I find a vintage Hindi movie on the 40 inch screen. In front of me is being played one of the oldest and adorable movies of the century, "DilwaleDulhania Le Jayenge". *Simran* is asking *Rahul* to betray her father and marry her. *Simran's* father is against love marriages; but *Rahul* refuses to marry her without her father's blessings, and he will have to convince her father for his will.

While I continue to watch the 'DDLJ' *again*, my eyes lay down on the brown hard-covered diary. It might be Rachel's personal diary. I extract her words from the buried memories in my mind. She skyped me, "I think I am beginning to like Erik. You know, I write every moment of mine spent together with him in my diary. My diary is a part of me, and when I feel blue, I turn the pages of my past to live my golden days again".

When Erik left her, she was broken into fragments. I consoled her as much as I could, sitting thousands of miles away from her. I think she loves me too. Our bond is indestructible.

I reach to pick up the diary, and scrutinize its dark front and back. I am not supposed to read anyone's personal life. I guess I will wait for her permission. I hide it in my luggage and lay back on the couch, drifting into a dreamless sleep this time.

I am awakened by the screeching sound of tires. I open the doors and lead a couple of men in black to upstairs. They transfer my father in a bag and chain him inside, leaving some space for him to breathe, and head to their vehicle.

"I am accompanying you", I say firmly, blocking their way outside.

They give a moment's gaze to me, and resume their job, without any other word. I lock the door behind me, and sit at the spacious backside of the ambulance, with my father lying in front of me, hidden inside the blue-colored plastic bag.

I loved him in my childhood. He was my loving and caring papa. My Superman, my real-life hero. I used to admire him. I loved to imitate him with my child eyes. I could have never imagined him to be the reason of my mother's death. I didn't accept him to turn from a hero to a monster.

On the one hour way, I continue to stare at his body. The ambulance comes to a halt and he is being carried to a building where he deserves to spend the rest of his life.

"Another insane patient", one of the men in black briefs the caretaker about the current situation. I am beckoned to stay outside, and since I don't have any other option, but to follow his orders, so I watch my father being taken away to the unknown part of the asylum.

I move out to the open. A green lawn is in front of me, and some patients rove from one end to another. I imagine papa in the midst of these people, acting the same way they are, lost in the different world from ours. I feel a grimace covering my face. This is the sin that I accept to bear my whole life.

I look upwards to the clear blue sky, covered with the patches of cloudy white color. *This is for you, mom. I avenged your death.*

I don't know whether she would be smiling, or regretting her decision of suicide, since her decision turned me into a sinner; but I know for sure, is that, my heart has found peace after a lifetime.

"Don't touch me. Stay away! Don't… Don't touch me. Don't touch…", one of the patients ran past me. I would be intrigued to study their minds and understand their history. What made them like they are now? I can use this weapon of knowledge of psychology against the so-called society of my nation; torturing others, poking at the misshapen of unfortunate people, avoiding the darkness in their own hearts.

"Let's go", the men in black come besides me.

I look towards the inside of the asylum, the others haven't yet returned. Reading my eyes, he says, "It's only me. Let's go".

"Take me to Mustafa", I say sternly.

He gives another moment's gaze and straightens his finger towards his car, matte black Ferrari Spider, beckoning me to ride with him.

I am a follower of Ferrari, always wanted to ride one, and dreamt of buying one. I pull up the door and ensconce in the ride of my dreams.

We arrive to our destination in just over half an hour. Followed by security checks, I am led to the white super corridor, we are moving in between the crowd of human puppets, dancing on the fingers of Mustafa.

"I didn't expect you to come see me", Mustafa says as he wraps me in his muscular embrace and his bulging out green veins.

I reply to his smile, "Wanted to visit the person who saved me from ruining my life".

Releasing me from his intimacy, he says, "So you going back to India?"

"Yeah! My job, here, is done. Now it's time for me to live in my mother nation with a peaceful heart", I reply as he offers me to sit on his imported dark-green leather couch, "Thank you, Mustafa. If you wouldn't have supported me at the right time, I would have worsened my life".

"Oh, don't be so modest, brother. I owed you, and now we are even. You saved my life; this is the least I could do for you", he pours me a glass of Scotch.

I shake my head, "I am sorry, but I can't join you for drink. I need to keep myself focused".

He gives way to a mature and understanding laughter, "Always mysterious!", and compliments me.

"Mustafa? I need one more green and blue pill", I ask, holding his free hand at place.

He looks at me, his eyes asking hundreds of questions, while his lips respond with just one question, "You will keep them safe, right?"

"I won't disappoint you", I answer.

His smile returns, "I know you won't".

He waves his hands to the men in black, ordering them to bring the things that I want. We have some casual talks and now, I am off on my way.

13.

"We are here", I exclaim.

"Thank you, Nipun, for *everything*", I can see tears forming in Romita's eyes as she gratifies.

I bring my head to touch hers, kiss her on her cheeks and reply, "You don't have to thank me. I followed my heart".

"I hope Rachel accepts you", she gives a tight hug and leaves for her home, leaving me dumbstruck.

I too hope so, Romita. She is the love of my life, and I have already delayed an era in exposing my feelings for her. I don't know whom she will choose, me, or Erik.

I grab my luggage, ready to leave Delhi airport and catch a bus to Shimla.

I close my eyes and take in the essence of Shimla, my hometown. "I missed you", I murmur to the place where I found my heart residing in the nature's lap. I run my left hand in my jacket's pocket, and take out one of the two pills, give it a glance and keep it back inside.

I call for an auto-rickshaw and recite my home's address to him. It's really *my* home now, having no place for a murderer.

"I am glad you made it alright", Rachel welcomes me , as if the universe is pouring its signs over me, solving the puzzle for me, telling me that she's meant to be with me.

"Me too", I kiss her on her cheek, inhaling all the loveliness of her presence.

"How did you manage to come here all by yourself?", Rachel asks, as her parents welcome me in my home.

"Romita helped me. She, too, was on her way to India", I answer.

Her perplexed face freezes for a minute, unable to choose her next question.

"And what about your father?", Mr. Cox asks.

"He is wherever he deserves to be", I answer in diplomacy.

"Where, Sonu?", Rachel asks.

"Also, his lab and experiments are also been taken care of", I ignore Rachel's questions, only to give way to more questions.

"But, how?", Rachel asks, on behalf of her answer-seeking parents as well.

"I destroyed it. Now, I am very tired. I should have some rest", before another question could be fired on me, I excuse myself to dwell on my next planned step.

It is rightly said, *there's no other place like home*, and for me, there's no home without Rachel in it. I discovered my love for Rachel after I met Romita. Romita was perfect for me, the kind of girl I could have fallen in love with, *if* I hadn't met Rachel and encountered her gabbling, her stubbornness, her biting her lips, her whispering blonde hair...

14.

"No!", I sit upright haunted by my same nightmare and the truth behind my dark soul. I thought it would stop after I would have avenged my mother's death. With my confused mind, I step outside my room to search for my best friend, carrying my heavy heart.

She is sitting in the old-looking dining hall, attached by a couch for watching television.

"There has been a huge blast in the northern part of California, destroying a whole laboratory filled with scientists from all over the world. People are mourning for their loss, while FBI has started their search for the culprits", a dark-haired and bearded man is coldly describing the status of my actions.

I didn't think it would come to this. All I wanted to do was to make this world a better place for Rachel and me to live.

"Raech?", she doesn't hear me in my first call, "Raech?", her focus is disrupted and her hair gives a sharp wave when she turns her head towards me.

"Nipun, look at this. The place where Gablet was made is destroyed! How did this happen? Who did this?", she starts mumbling and she is again lost in her thoughts, wondering about my past wordings.

As I stare at her, gathering all my courage to confront her, she asks with her face drowned in the doubt of my sacredness, "Did you do this?"

"I need to talk to you", I whisper and start moving towards my room, definitely followed by the love of my life.

"Sit here", a humble guilty lover asks his best friend to take a seat on his bed.

"I need you to listen to everything I want to say, before you react. Can you do that for me?", I ask, taking my place on her feet.

She nods, her forehead reflecting the confusion of her soul.

"I love you Rachel Cox. I have loved you from the beginning, and I have known my feelings for you when I was 14 years old. I never developed the guts to confront my feelings to you, and I know, now it's too late for that. Still, I don't want my life to end without you knowing that I have been in true love with you; so true, that I couldn't fall in love with any girl other than you", she opens her mouth to say, but my order doesn't let her, so I continue.

"I have all the answers you need. But before I tell you everything, you need to make a promise to me that you won't hate me. Will you?", I ask, holding out her hands in mine.

"I promise I won't hate you ever", she replies, with the surety defining her whole life.

I smile and continue, "I am the reason your father had to suffer the consequence of insanity. I am the reason he found that green pill, but I didn't intend him to find that. It was meant to be taken by my papa. Since my mum has left me, there is not a night that goes by when I don't have her dreams, jumping from that well, where I could have saved her, and I didn't. *I* know how I used to live with my papa under the same roof. I wanted to choke him every night. Yes Raech, I am not a good person. I wanted to avenge the death of my mum, I wanted her soul to rest in peace by making my papa suffer, and I almost killed him, when I encountered with my friend Mustafa, and he told me about this Gablet. He and a group of psychologists experimented on almost every breed of animal, the ones we saw in that eerie lab, and found that all reacted with one thing common, they found peace within themselves, and when one finds peace, you can easily read one's mind. This is what they intended to do with human minds; but as we can see, they failed. Instead of bringing peace to them, the pill destroyed the humans' sanity.

"What I did in California after you left? I gave him the green pill when he was with me in your room. I escorted my unconscious papa to an asylum and left to meet Mustafa. Mustafa is the one who created the green pill. I rescued all the animals, before I bombed that place. Then healed Romita by giving her the blue pill, escorted her to Delhi airport and here I am", I wait for her to take in the contents of my true self. I have never shown my dark side to her before, in the

193

fear of losing her, but now I know that if I want her to love me back, then she needs to love my true self, and not the pretentious one.

She stands and walks towards the door, "I need sometime alone".

I sit on my bed and put the left-alone green pill from my pocket. I am unsure of its fortune, and Rachel is the only one with the power to decide my fate.

I lay back and stare at the roof, plain and old dabbed with dark patches, like my soul. I remember the first time I saw Rachel, she was standing beneath an autumn tree, all red and orange. Looking at her at that moment was to witness a rising sun in the twilight.

I remember the time when she fell in love with my black beauty, Sam. She used to share all her problems with the shining black horse, and I used to eavesdrop behind the window and stare at her glowing eyes.

There were times where my feelings tried to explode and reach out to her, but the fear in me subjugated them. I regret not confronting to her sooner, because now, I am darker and deeper than before.

If she rejects me, I won't be upset, because I am stark aware of the person I am turned into. I am ready to accept her answer and choose my future.

"Nipun", a voice calls to me. I sit up to face my crying best friend. I can't let her cry.

She comes near and kisses me on my cheeks, her tears wetting my face, her smell sweet and toxic.

"I am still going to be by your side forever, but, I can't leave Erik. I am sorry. I love you both. Only if I would have known before, only if I wouldn't have gone so far for Erik, this would have been different", she cries and her weak soul falls on the floor.

I follow her emotions and sit in front of her, "Please don't cry. I totally understand. It's my fault. Don't let yourself bear the pain of my doings", I wipe her tears and show my smiling face, "I wish a happy future to both of you".

"RACHEL!", I hear her mother calling to her, "It's time to go".

Rachel looks through my eyes, "We are going back to California".

I stand up and pull her, becoming her strength for the last time.

After a heart-aching farewell, I walk towards my barn and stare at the life-turning well, "I am sorry, mum".

I take out the green pill, open my grip to observe its shiny colors floating above my palm, and let it slide through my slippery human throat.

www.ingramcontent.com/pod-product-compliance
Lightning Source LLC
Chambersburg PA
CBHW021147130626
46554CB00005B/1700